RESERVE MY CURVES

HE STILL BELONGS TO ME

B.M. Hardin

ISBN-13: 978-0692480823

ISBN-10: 069248082X

2015©Savvily Published LLC

Dedication

This book is dedicated to a special superstar reader, Farrah Clark Watson.

Thank you for all of your support and for following me on my writing journey. It is truly a blessing to have a supporter like you in my corner. Thank you!

Special thanks to Sparkle Nicole for gracing the cover with her curves! Thank you!

Photographer: Carrie Smith of CCMG (Conceited Curves Model Management) Amazing photos and thank you as well!

<u>Acknowledgements</u>

First and foremost, I want to thank my Heavenly Father for my talents and my gifts and each and every story that he has placed in me.

It is an honor and a privilege to be living my dream and walking in my purpose and for that I am forever thankful.

Also to all of my family, friends, critiques, supporters, readers and everyone else, thank you for believing in me and allowing me to share my gifts with you.

Your support truly means the world to me!

B.M. Hardin

Reserve My Curves 2: He Still Belongs to Me

Chapter ONE

Did he just say what I thought he'd said?

And who in the hell was *his* husband?

Unsure of what to say next or how to respond, I just stood there and didn't say a word.

This was a joke.

I mean, he just had to be joking.

Carmen's stupid ass probably put him up to this.

The man still looked a bit tensed, but I could tell that he had a whole lot to say.

And I was all ears.

"I found out that he had been screwing you, often, and the fact that he's even attracted to women took me by surprise. I had no idea. He'd told me that he had never so much as touched a woman before. But I'm telling you right here, and right now, don't sleep with my husband again. Or you will be sorry," he threatened me.

The more and more he talked, I could hear in his voice just how serious he was, so I was sure that this wasn't a joke.

He was serious and he meant business.

And it definitely made me feel some kind of way.

I mean, sure, I would prefer to only deal with straight men, but Carmen and this business was all about the money so who knows what kind of men I had been laying down with.

The only for sure things that I knew about a client, most of the time, were that he had money and had a penis.

Oh, and that *he* was horny.

Everything else was pretty much up in the air.

Feeling perplexed, I felt the need to take a seat, but instead of sitting next to him, I sat in a chair across from him.

He looked at me with pure hatred in his eyes.

And I could also see just a little bit of jealousy.

But I guess I had this coming.

In this type of business, a few things were destined to happen.

I had come to terms with that a long time ago.

"Who is your husband?" I asked him hesitantly.

He stared at me as though he didn't understand why I was asking him that question.

But the truth was that his husband could damn near be anybody.

Basically he, whoever he was, was just one in the number of men that I'd been with.

Since I no longer cared about sleeping with married men, I couldn't even begin to count how many I'd actually been with in just a short period of time.

Let alone name them.

Hell, he would be lucky if I even knew or recognized his name at all.

Most clients went with fake identities for just a little extra security.

Not all of them, but most.

I waited patiently for the gentleman to answer my question.

Finally, he did.

"My husband is…"

I took a deep breath.

"Nolan," he said.

What?

What did he just say?

Nolan?

My dead sister baby's daddy and my little side piece Nolan?

Oh hell no!

"I'm sorry, what did you say?"

Without hesitating, he repeated himself.

"I said Nolan is my husband," he repeated.

I frowned and shook my head.

What?

How?

When?

Huh?

How in the hell was Nolan *his* husband?

I was shocked that this wasn't hotel related.

Who would have thought that this had something to do with what I was doing in my personal life?

And furthermore, how in the hell did this man even know that I worked at the hotel?

And how did he know about the thirteenth floor?

And wait a minute…Nolan was, well is, gay?

Huh!

I would have never, ever, guessed it!

Nolan was just so attentive when he touched me and some of the things that he'd done to me couldn't even be put into words.

I just didn't get that vibe from him.

But he was married...

And to a man?

Since when?

He just *had* a wife not too long ago.

So, how was *he* his husband?

I was so confused!

"Okay, so you have to break this down for me. How in the hell are you Nolan's husband when he just buried his wife just a little while ago?" I asked him.

Immediately I could tell that I had just broken some news to him that had broken his heart.

He looked at me as though he didn't believe me.

"Wife?" he asked.

"Yes, he had a wife."

"When? How? And he buried her? So she's dead?"

"Yes. She killed herself, after she killed my sister for having an affair with Nolan; her husband or your husband," I responded confusedly.

I was mind boggled.

"We ran off to Vegas about a month ago and got married. After two years, he'd said that he was finally ready," he said.

"That's a bunch of bull. He was married to the woman that killed my sister because she was carrying his baby."

"Baby? What baby?"

Oh my, he didn't even know about the baby?

What the hell did Nolan have going on over there!

And how in the world was he pulling it all off?

"Nolan has a son, my nephew. I raise him part of the time and he takes him the other half of the time. Where are you when he has him?"

"That's a good question. He has never told me about a son or even brought him home for me to meet him. I'm confused. Who in the hell hides a baby? Or a wife? Well, a *used to be* wife."

He looked more than frustrated.

Hell he wasn't the only one.

Nolan and I had been humping like dogs in heat, but it was safe to say that he would never touch me again.

I guess that's what I get for being so damn trifling.

"How did you know that we were having sex?" I asked him curiously.

"I went through his phone. The nasty text messages between the two of you almost made me catch a *charge*. Funny, I never saw any messages about this so-called son of his though. Anyway, I got your name and number and I had a friend of mine to trace it and pull up everything that I needed to know about you. I'd come by your house one day and just as I was pulling up, you were dressed for work and getting into the car. So, I followed you to the hotel. From trying to find a parking space, I was a few steps behind you, but when I entered the hotel, you were nowhere in sight. I asked the front desk for you and a few minutes later, an exquisitely dressed woman came to tell me that you were on vacation. But I knew that she was lying because I'd just seen you go in there. So, since she was lying that could only mean one thing…she was hiding something. So, I did a little more digging and after a few conversations, I found out the hotel's dirty, little secret. It wasn't all that hard actually. When you have a little money, and get to talking to someone else that may or may not have a little bit more money than you do, it's not hard for a few things to slip out here and there, that involves *inappropriately* spending money, rather than making it. So, *she* and I met again, but this time by referral. I'm not sure if she recognized me or not, but I did the necessary to get on this floor. And bam, what do you know. Just like that, I was face to face with my husband's mistress," he said.

Wow!

And well of course he had money.

He wouldn't be here if he didn't.

"It was just sex. I was already working on keeping a distance from Nolan anyway. This makes it a whole lot easier. Of course I didn't know about you. But now that I do, he most definitely won't be touching me again," I promised him.

"He had a baby with your *real* sister?"

I nodded.

"Scandalous," he said to me and shook his head.

He was right.

I'd always known that I was dead wrong for sleeping with Nolan, but I couldn't help myself.

Oh, but now, not screwing him was going to be a piece of cake!

"So what now? Do you confront him? Or do I let him know that I know the truth about him?"

"No. I've found out that he is a liar and a cheater so there's really not much left to say. To be honest, I know that he uses me. I know that he probably just married me for the money. But at least I have someone. At least he's there. I'd always suspected that he was having an affair…just not with a woman. But it all makes sense now as to why I could never come to his house and little things like that. He'd said that it was because his mother lived with him and that she didn't approve of his lifestyle, when obviously, it was because he was really living with his wife. But I don't need you to say or do a thing…except stop screwing him," he said.

At that moment, as uncomfortable as it all was, I realized how in life and in so many relationships, people settle.

People were willing to put up with the unthinkable just to hear the words I love you.

They settle because they're comfortable or because they don't want to be alone.

Why is that?

Why is it so hard to accept defeat or to stand up and say that this doesn't work for me anymore and I am no longer happy?

I guess it's just one of the many mysteries of life.

But one thing was for sure and that was that you always have to expect the unexpected.

Nothing in life was ever truly guaranteed.

Silas crossed my mind at that very moment, and I thought of how lucky I was to have him.

It was time for me to take some chances and that included finally becoming someone's wife.

The gentleman and I chatted for a while longer and I tried to give him some kind of advice if that's what you wanted to call it.

My life wasn't perfect but for the most part it seemed as though he was really listening to what I had to say.

I surely wouldn't take much advice from an overpriced prostitute if I was in his shoes, but it didn't seem to bother him and it sure as hell never seemed to stop most of my other clients who was always venting about their personal problems and issues.

Lots of them wanted to talk about things that I didn't give a damn about.

But on any given day, it was better than lying on my back or getting on my knees.

Believe me, selling ass was exhausting!

Finally the gentleman cracked a smile and his next statement caught me by surprise.

"I've never been with a woman. But I can see why my husband had a hard time keeping his hands to himself," he said.

I looked at him confused.

Was he coming on to me?

Oh Hell-to-the-No!

I would definitely stop sleeping with Nolan but my goodness, if he wanted to sample the curves too, now that would be asking for too damn much!

But luckily he didn't.

After a few more words, he was gone.

I lingered around the room as though I was cleaning it up and as soon as I opened the door, Carmen was standing there.

She just stood there.

After a while she moved to the side and I headed to the lounge.

Carmen followed me.

"What?" I asked with an attitude as I turned around to face her.

"I was his first wife, so I'll always have his heart," she said.

I rolled my eyes.

Really?

She really wanted to continue talking about Silas?

And newsflash, he hated her!

"Well, I have his dick and his bank card, so what you saying? That's my two to your one. So, I still win. But, I'm sure his heart belongs to me too. But if thinking that makes you feel better, go right ahead," I said to her.

Stupid ass.

Carmen stared at me as if she wanted to take off her earrings and rumble with me, but instead she walked away.

I could only imagine the hell that she'd given her sister, though I guess she couldn't really be blamed for that one.

Maybe she thought that with her sister dead, that there was some small chance that she and Silas could've reconciled, and I was in the way.

I had no idea what was going on in that crazy head of hers, but for her sake, she had better leave me the hell alone, or she would find her feelings hurt every single time.

The rest of the day went by with a breeze and I headed to Carmen's office on my way out to pick up my money for the day.

She wasn't in her upstairs office, so I headed down the elevator.

To my surprise she wasn't there either.

But I was sure that she wasn't too far.

As I started to head out, I noticed that on the back of her closed office door she had an envelope taped to the back of it that said: "Bitch a.k.a Envy".

Believe me when I say that I was going to whoop her ass if it was the last thing that I do!

And I meant that!

I snatched the envelope down and opened it just to make sure that my money was inside.

I wondered where she'd gone but I prayed that something bad would happen to her wherever she was.

Then I would be contract *and* Carmen free.

Now that would be something to smile about.

Wishful thinking…

***

I smiled at Horizon as she played with the baby.

I'd always hoped to give her a sibling one day, and I was glad that in a way, more or less, I had.

I mean she had a *real* sister, somewhere, but it wasn't the same.

But with the baby, now, my little family felt complete.

Well, except that Nolan was still in the picture.

I was still trying my best not to let him know that I knew his secret.

And it was so damn hard!

I'd always been so good with keeping secrets, especially my own, but biting my tongue on this one was difficult for me.

He had gone too far and I could barely even look him in the face without wanting to smack him.

Look, whatever a person chooses to do in their life, was their decision.

Whoever a person chooses to be was their choice.

I wasn't their judge or their jury, but be upfront about your preferences.

Seriously, I couldn't stand a down low brotha'!

What you walking around lying to people for?

But I swear Nolan just seemed to be in love with the *kitty cat*, so it was still shocking to me and a bit hard for me to believe.

But even I knew that people could hide anything if they put forth enough effort.

Whatever it was, I didn't want any parts of it.

I'd told him that same day that we could never get down on that level again.

Since my days at the hotel were counting down, I was looking forward to a life of no more secrets and no more lies.

But Nolan wasn't too fond of my sudden decision.

He was definitely starting to act a little crazy since I'd cut him off from the booty.

He was constantly questioning me about it and he was showing signs of obsession.

Hell, if I wasn't mistaken, a few nights I'd looked out the window and seen a car similar to his a few houses up.

I could only hope that he wasn't about to act a fool.

After all, he didn't have the right to.

I'll admit that sex with him had been good; wrong, but so damn good.

But we both knew that we could have never been more than sex for the sake of Tia.

Finding out that he had a husband just put the icing on the cake.

Just as the last thought crossed my mind, Nolan's name appeared on my phone.

"Hey, what is he doing?"

"Playing with Horizon."

"I miss him…and I miss you," Nolan said.

I knew that was coming.

"Nolan, look, we can't do what we've being doing anymore. It's not right. It's not right to Tia. It's disrespectful. And it's definitely not right to Silas. And since I plan to be planning a wedding soon, let's just stop this now, before things get out of hand," I said to him, still making sure that I didn't mention his secret.

There were already enough issues in my life and it was in my best interest to stop adding to the list.

Nolan sat for a long while, without saying a word.

"Okay Envy," he finally said and with a few more words, he said his goodbyes.

Well, at least he hadn't reacted like he had previously. Maybe it was all starting to sink in.

Whatever the reason was, whatever we had, was over.

Sooner or later if I hadn't done it, I was sure that he would have had to.

Maybe.

Then again, men always wanted or tried to have it all.

At least, that's the way that I saw it.

As the kids continued to play, I allowed my mind to take me to a place that I hadn't been in quite some time.

I went back to a time of my early years with Horizon's daddy, and my first love, Keymar.

I thought about how much I'd loved him and I also thought about how I would do anything in the world to make him happy, back then.

Even if that meant watching him have sex with someone else.

I couldn't believe that I'd forced myself to forget about the ordeal but for some reason, I remembered it now so clearly.

It was as though it'd only happened yesterday.

It's sad when you have so many secrets, that you actually manage to forget about a few of them; especially the ones that hurt you the most.

Anyway, Keymar and I had just moved into our first place together and it was his birthday.

I was so in love with him that if he'd told me to jump off of a bridge I probably would have.

I'm sure I would've.

I did everything he told me to do, when he told me to do it; except for this one time.

He'd asked me for a threesome and at first, I'd agreed.

It was his birthday and that's what he'd wanted.

He'd said that it was a fantasy of his and my dumb ass thought that I was obligated to give him a night that he would never forget.

I thought that I was going to be able to do it, I really did.

I was young.

I was sexy.

And I was in love.

But when he'd brought the woman into our bedroom, at the last minute, I backed out.

I just couldn't do it.

But…Keymar could.

With or without me, he still wanted to have sex with her.

And guess what, I let him.

I couldn't believe that I'd forgotten about it all.

How could I have forgotten such disrespect?

Thinking about it now, I felt so hurt and angry.

Keymar had told me that if I loved him, I would either join in, or let him have sex with her so that he could get it out of his system.

And like a fool, I believed him.

And the craziest part of all was that I sat there and I watched.

I watched the entire time and didn't say one word.

All I could think about was that I loved him and he loved me, and I just wanted him to be happy.

But the truth was---that wasn't love.

That was stupidity.

I was young, naïve and stupid and I should have dropped Keymar's ass like a bad habit; right after I'd beat him in the back with a baseball bat.

That's what I should have done.

But I hadn't.

I hadn't done anything.

He'd promised that it was just something that young guys wanted to do and he swore that from that day forward that as long as I gave him the *goods* whenever he asked for them, I would never have to worry about another woman.

But of course that had been a lie too.

And for years, I'd stayed with him and bowed down to him and done everything under the sun for him because I thought that that's what you did when you loved someone.

But I couldn't have been more wrong.

Shaking away the thoughts of my past, I was almost in tears.

The memory of it all had been hidden for so long and so deep in my mind and heart, that I felt all of the emotions that I'd felt on that very day and then some.

How could he have done something like that to me?

And with the whole baby mama coming out of the blue, I figured that Keymar had probably been with plenty of women while we were together and I wondered if he'd ever really loved me at all.

Nope, I was sure that he didn't.

I was sure that whatever we'd had wasn't love.

At least not on his end.

But now what Silas showed me; now that was love.

It just had to be.

And I wasn't going to do anything, other than what I was already doing at the hotel, to mess up what we shared.

That's why Nolan's ass had to go!

Later on that evening, once Silas was home and the kids were in bed, I made love to Silas like never before.

I tried my best to show him with ever curve of my body just how much I loved him and appreciated him for all of the things that he'd done for me and the kids on a regular basis.

He truly was a great guy, a little mysterious, maybe even questionable at times, but great nonetheless, and I could feel that his love for me was real.

And I would do anything to keep it.

Now all I had to do was get away from the hotel and things from that point on were going to be just fine.

I was sure of it.

***

"Silas what are you doing?" I laughed and clapped my hands together.

He was standing in the doorway of the bedroom, dressed like a cowboy; minus the shirt.

He was all oiled up and his body was glowing brighter than the stars that led the slaves to freedom in the midst of the candlelight.

Silas threw the cowboy hat on the bed beside me and smiled.

I was giggling and laughing like never before.

It was just the little things that he did.

He was always doing something just to put a smile on my face.

"Envy? Are you going let me *ride* that *donkey*?" He managed to ask before bursting into laughter.

He was so stupid, yet so damn cute, and all at the same time.

And I was turned all the way on by it!

Surprisingly, next, he started to dance.

He danced towards me, though no music was playing and I damn near ripped off the rest of the cowboy outfit once he was within my reach.

He was still in character and he whispered naughty things in my ear that damn near drove me crazy.

I practically begged him to stop talking and forced him to *enter* me.

Once he *filled* me up, I was ready for the ride!

And I was going to enjoy every second of it...

"You were *reserved* for the entire day, but he isn't here yet, so I guess you can hang out in your room or do whatever whores like you do, until he gets here," Carmen said without so much as looking me in my face.

She was being so disrespectful!

And that statement should have offended every *executive maid* within listening range, but none of them said a word or even acted as though they'd heard her comment.

I wanted to take of my shoe and throw it at the back of her head as she walked away, but she was going to get what was coming to her.

It was obvious that she was just taking shots because she was jealous of what Silas and I had.

At this point, I was sure she hated me.

It was all in her voice but I was glad that we were finally on the same page.

The feelings were mutual.

I couldn't stand her.

If she was on fire, I wouldn't even spit on her to try to help her out.

But she was just going to have to get over herself, get over Silas and move on with her life because I was definitely moving forward with mine…with Silas by my side.

But on a serious note, I wondered why she was still so jealous about him after all these years.

Or maybe it was just the fact that he was with me.

Yeah, I was sure that was it.

Maybe she thought a woman like me didn't deserve him.

But that was her problem, not mine.

Since I hadn't had much sleep because of Silas and his little show, once inside Room 313, I decided to take a little nap.

But just as I started to drool, I heard the room door open.

Carmen said a few words to the client and then stuck her head in.

"Slut get up," I heard her say.

I was about to call her everything but a child of God, but just as I opened my mouth to speak, he appeared.

Taking a deep breath and rubbing my eyes, I stared at him.

My first thought was…eww!

Something about him just seemed off.

He just looked weird and not to mention, that he was butt ugly!

He had a nice body and all; tall, broad shoulders and he was even a mouthwatering chocolate complexion, but he just wasn't much of a looker.

I was totally disappointed that he'd reserved me for my entire shift.

Now I had to spend hours with someone that I could barely even look at.

Carmen closed the door as he came closer to me.

I smiled in an attempt to hide my disappointment as he sat on the other side of the bed.

I could tell that this was his first time.

He just sat there, looking at the floor.

He wasn't saying anything so, I guessed that it was time for me to play my part and do my job.

I was hoping that he didn't want to do anything strange, because ugly and strange just wasn't a good combination.

"I'm Envy," I said.

"I know who you are," he said with a sort of dry tone.

Ugh, he even *talked* ugly!

Oh my, this was going to be a long day!

"So, I'm all yours, all day. So do you want me to go change into something specific? Since you reserved me, I wanted to wait and go off of whatever it was that you had in mind," I said trying to sound sexy.

I stood up so that he could get a good look at me and my curves but he didn't seem all that interested.

I smiled at him, but he frowned at me.

What's his problem?

I came closer to him, but at my touch he flinched and then he stood to his feet.

Without speaking, he opened his blazer and there it was...a silver badge.

He was the police?

Oh hell no!

****

Chapter TWO

I backed away from him and I sat down in one of the chairs with my mouth hanging wide open.

It seemed as though showing his badge had given him some kind of ego boost or something, because suddenly he was talking non-stop.

He went on to explain that he was an undercover cop; a detective actually.

Uh oh!

His name was Detective Wiley…but Detective Ugly would have been a better fit.

"Envy, we've been watching you for quite some time now. We've known about this hotel operation for a while but with so many people on *their* payroll, so to speak, bringing them down hasn't been easy. But we finally got some big leagues in our corner, and finally we got the greenlight to build this case. Being as to that I'm here, on the thirteenth floor, supposedly paying for sex, it's clear that we were right. But we need more. We need the people at the top of this chain and all of those that are involved along the way. That includes Carmen, her boss, and even her boss's boss. And hell if *he* has a boss, we want him too. We want them all. You're the only one of the girls that we have ever seen out in public with Carmen, so we can only assume that you guys have some kind of relationship or type of friendship," he said.

Immediately, I shook my head.

"Oh no, we hate each other. You have it all wrong."

"Haven't you guys gone out to dinner after hours?"

"Yes, but that was some time ago. Things are very different between us these days."

"Didn't she just attend your sister's funeral?"

Damn.

I guess he wasn't playing when he said that he had been watching me.

"Yes, but…"

"Look, if you help us, of course you'll walk away from this with your freedom. We won't press any charges against you. Yes, you're facing them too even though you are a small fish in a big pond, you're still apart of this. But I can help you, if you help me. But if you don't, you will go down with everyone else on this sinking ship."

No! I couldn't go to jail. I had Horizon, and the baby to take care of.

Who would take care of them if I was gone?

They needed me.

With two months barely left to go, here comes something like this.

My contract was almost up and I was almost through.

I was almost out of here and I couldn't have anything keeping me around even a day longer than I had to be.

But clearly, in order to keep my freedom, my cooperation was going to be a must, I suppose.

"They know a lot of people. They have connections everywhere. It's going to be impossible to bring them down. It's going to be impossible to even get your case in front of a judge. A lot of them are involved in this too," I said to him softly.

Carmen had briefly given me a rundown when I first started of some of the higher connections that they had and to be honest, in my opinion, this detective was in way over his head.

I didn't have even a little bit of confidence in him that he was going to succeed in bringing down this operation.

There was too much power involved.

But there was a slight possibility that he actually did pull it all off, and if so, I needed my freedom.

I hated Carmen so throwing her under the bus to save myself was going to be my pleasure, but I knew that it was going to be one hell of a task.

And I didn't have long to do it.

"You let us worry about all of that. We just need you to get in as close as possible and find out as much information as you can about the operation. We need names, connections, and contacts. We know it's not going to be easy but we are going to have to try our best to get as much as we can. This is bigger than prostitution and the smaller things that you may have in mind. We believe that there could be murders and maybe even mob ties to this operation. We're not for sure, that's why we need your help," he said.

Damn it!

I definitely didn't like the sound of possible murders or even possible mob dealings being in the mix.

Was he trying to get me killed?

I don't care what they tell you, somebody, somehow, always finds out who the rat is, and if I take his offer, the rat was going to be me.

Oh my, why me?

But I knew that I didn't have a choice; not if I wanted to be there for my babies.

I could tell by the way that he talked that he was going forward, with or without me agreeing to help him.

So, in other words, I had to do this; which meant that I now had to be nice to Carmen and I had to find a way to make her trust me, in hopes of finding out enough information to guarantee my freedom.

He'd made it crystal clear that Carmen was the key.

But even if I tried to fake it or tried to establish a newfound phony friendship with her, at this point, I was sure that she wouldn't want to be friends or have any type of personal dealings with me; especially since it was obvious that she despised me for being with Silas.

So how was I supposed to get close to her?

Leaving Silas wasn't an option; but then again, that was nothing that a little lie couldn't fix or cover up.

Yes, maybe that would work.

Maybe I could lie to her about my relationship with Silas.

What better to bring two women together than bashing and talking down about an "ex"?

And I was sure that Carmen would be all ears to hear that Silas did something as foul to me as he'd done to her.

It was a brilliant idea!

"Okay, so where do I start? What do I do?"

"You start digging. You start asking questions. You have to make them trust you; Carmen and the clients. If they trust you, someone is bound to make a mistake, and start talking. You just don't know what one of the men that you've been sleeping with knows. Hell, you never know, one of them could very well be the man in charge or maybe one of them knows who the *boss* is. Somebody knows something," he said.

I listened attentively for the next hour or so.

It was obvious that I was going to have to board this train and hope for the best.

It was the only choice that I had.

After he was done talking and since he'd ordered me for the entire day, with nothing left to do, he fell asleep sitting in a chair and I stretched out for a nap on the bed.

He had to stay around so that Carmen didn't get suspicious.

Briefly I'd wondered who else was on his team. Somebody had to be working with him in order for him to even be on the thirteenth floor.

But of course he hadn't gone into details about that.

Hours later, he woke me up and after making sure that I had all of his contact information, he exited the room.

Soon after, I followed.

Instead heading to the lounge, I prepared to leave.

"I wonder what Silas would think of you if he knew your little secret. What would he think of you if he knew that you spent hours most days, lying on your back? Anyway, here's what you earned for a whore's day of work," Carmen said and dropped the envelope full of money to the floor in front of me, just as I reached out my hand.

Please keep me near the cross!

Somebody, anybody, pray for me!

I know damn well she didn't just drop some money on the floor like I was some two-dollar *hoe* or something.

I was trying my best to keep my cool, especially since I'd recently found out that I was going to have to be nice to her, but enough is enough!

"I don't have long to be here you know that right? But I tell you what, on the day that my contract is up, I'm going to drag your ass all over this office. And that's a promise that you can take to the bank," I said to her as I stepped over the envelope and walked out of her office.

Technically, I hadn't earned the money any damn way, and I sure as hell didn't need it.

I had to take a few deep breaths to calm myself down.

That chick had my *trigger finger* itching and that was nothing but the truth!

Being nice to her just wasn't going to work.

Detective Wiley just might have to find him someone else to do the job.

If I had to do it, worrying about going to jail for prostitution and whatever the other charges were, would be the least of my problems.

I was sure that messing around with Carmen, I would be going to jail for murder.

***

"Envy, I just want to take you home with me," one of my regular clients said.

The things that the idiots said on a regular basis!

"Oh really, I don't think your wife would like that," I laughed in Mr. Ben's face, but he didn't crack a smile.

Mr. Ben was a fairly new client of mine, since it wasn't all that long ago that I'd started sleeping with the married men. But since his first time on *Envy's rodeo*, he came to see me once or twice a week.

He was biracial and in his late forties.

He never talked much about what he did for a living, but I knew that he had a whole lot of money and he didn't mind giving it to me.

He was also the rich client that had *requested* me and had gotten a glimpse of me on the bottom floor, when I was just a regular maid.

He was the reason that Carmen had initially offered me the *promotion* to come up to the thirteenth floor in the first place.

"Oh, my marriage is the only thing standing in the way? Well, we can handle that situation. Just say the word and she's *gone*," he said with a straight face.

What?

If he didn't get his crazy ass out of here!

"Mr. Ben, now you know that wouldn't be right."

"Says who? That's your opinion, not mine. Oh, I get it. You're just using me for my money, just like everybody else?"

Is he serious?

He was the one paying for *my* pussy, so if anyone should feel used in this situation, it should be me.

But because I was becoming extremely freaked out with the conversation, and because I had the detective's words in my mind about getting my client's to really trust me, I told him what he wanted to hear, shifted his focus back to sex and then satisfied him with my mouth just the way that he liked it.

I swear things and the people on the thirteenth floor were getting crazier by the day, which was a sure sign that it was time for me to get the hell away from this place.

I'd been walking around on egg shells at the hotel since being approached by the ugly detective.

I always felt like someone knew what I was up to or like someone was always watching me; which of course the detective was watching all of us.

He'd explained that in order to start building a case against Carmen and all of those in charge, I had to get in close and find some things that would be deemed useful.

They wanted hard proof.

They already knew that they were paying as many people as they could to be in their corner, so they needed hard and strong evidence.

He wanted the name of the head honcho or honchos in charge. I mean the ones at the very top of the operation. He wanted their sidekicks, other names, investors, financial information, and anything that could directly tie the lawyers, doctors, judges and celebrities to the hotel.

They wanted it all and they expected me to get it.

The question was, how in the hell was I supposed to do that?

Though I wasn't exactly sure of how to go about it all, it was clear that it had to be done.

So, Carmen had to become a top priority, more or less.

I really and truly disliked her, so trying to communicate with her on a personal level was going to be hell.

But this was the only way to keep myself out of trouble so I was going to have to figure it out, one day at a time.

After I was done servicing Mr. Ben, I tried to ask a few questions, but he didn't really much to say.

Hell all he wanted to talk about was taking me home with him and stupid stuff like that.

I'll try questioning him again when he was in his right frame of mind.

"You seem a little on edge about something," Silas said to me once I was home later on that evening.

I was off from the hotel for the next three days, and I planned on using that time to get my mind together.

Of course I couldn't tell Silas the truth about what was really bothering me.

"Oh no, I'm fine. I'm just a little tired that's all," I said to him.

Silas smiled and placed my feet into his lap.

He began to massage them and I closed my eyes to relax and focus on the feeling.

He was saying all the right things; sweet things, flattering things. He said all of the things that a woman wanted to hear, especially after a long day of "work".

But that moment was short lived.

The ringing of the doorbell told us that the baby was home.

Instantly, I smiled.

When the baby was gone with Nolan, I missed him like crazy.

I figured that once I was done with the hotel, I would keep him all week and Nolan could just get him on the weekends.

Things between Nolan and I were still weird but since I'd put it all on the table, we hadn't had sex or even come close to crossing that line.

Actually, he was a lot more nonchalant.

We only spoke about the baby and that worked just fine for me.

I sent Silas to the door to get the baby so that I didn't have to face Nolan, but my little plan failed.

"Envy I need to talk to you," Nolan shouted.

For some reason, I got a bad feeling all at once.

I headed to the door to see that Silas wasn't holding the baby.

As a matter of fact, neither was Nolan.

"Where's the baby?" I asked him.

Nolan just looked at me.

I could tell that there was still some frustration, on his end, but for the most part, I was more concerned about where the baby was.

"Where's the baby?"

"He's fine. I came to tell you that I'm not bringing him back," Nolan said.

My heart broke instantly and it felt as though it had been stomped on repeatedly.

For a second I could barely breathe.

"What do you mean you're not bringing him back?" Silas asked him, since I was finding it hard to speak.

"He's my son. I'm on the birth certificate and I've been seeking legal counsel. I'm moving away with him. I just thought that I would stop by to let you know," Nolan said.

What?

This could not be happening!

He couldn't do that…could he?

"Nolan, please. Please don't do this," I begged.

His face was so angry.

It was obvious that he was doing this to get back at me but this seemed a bit extreme.

"I can't be around you. I can't continue to see you," Nolan said and then he turned and walked away.

Against my better judgement, I ran after him and tried to reason with him, but he wouldn't listen.

He stood at the car door as I cried and begged him but he didn't seem to care.

"Nolan, let's go," a voice from the car said.

I looked in the backseat to see if the baby was there but when I didn't see him, I checked to see who was speaking from the passenger side of the car.

At the sight of her, I almost passed out.

It was Marie; the woman from the bus…Keymar's *other* child's mother.

"What? Wait? You know her?" I asked Nolan.

He looked at me as though I'd asked a stupid question.

"Yes, we're cousins. She's one of the one's that's been helping me with the baby," Nolan said.

Well I'll be damned!

If it wasn't one hell of a small world!

I shook my head and turned my attention back to Nolan who was now trying to figure out whether to listen to my voice, or to the voice that belonged to Marie.

I hadn't seen her again since she'd told me that the man that I had been madly in love with had cheated on me and had a baby with her.

Of course there hadn't been any exchange of information, so our daughters were growing up without getting to know each other.

Thinking about it, it didn't seem fair to the girls, but that wasn't important at this very moment.

Finally, Nolan pushed away from me, got into his car and drove away.

I stood there in tears, as I watched his car until it was out of sight.

Was this really happening?

Was he really trying to take the baby away from me?

"Envy?" Silas called out to me.

I'd forgotten that he was even there.

Slowly, I turned around to face him.

"Did something happen between you two that I need to know about?"

Damn it.

Nolan had made the remarks on purpose.

How would he have felt if I'd blurted out his little secret?

"No. He wanted more but I told him that I couldn't do that to you or Tia," I lied.

Silas studied my face for a second.

Now, I was crying uncontrollably so even if he wanted to see something, through my tears he wasn't going to be able to find it.

So, instead, he walked closer to me, and embraced me.

"Don't worry about a thing. I got you," Silas said and I knew that he meant just what he'd said.

****

Chapter THREE

"Hi," I said to Carmen as nice as I possibly could.

It was going to be so hard to be nice to her, but I didn't have a choice.

She looked at me as though I was a stranger on the street.

Once she turned her back to me, without saying a word, I knew that she had no intention on being casual, so I had to find a different approach.

"You were right about Silas," I said behind her.

At the sound of that, she turned around so fast that just watching her almost made me dizzy.

Well duh, at Silas's name, she was all ears.

Of course in reality, Silas and I were just fine, but she didn't have to know that.

"He's just not who I thought that he was," I said to her now that I had her full attention.

"I told you. I told you. What did he do?" she said and followed me to the lounge.

I fed her some bogus lie about Silas cheating on me and I told her that I'd called off the wedding.

Luckily Silas had taken my ring to have it cleaned, so it wasn't on my finger and everything looked legit.

Now I was just going to have to remember to take it off each day before coming into the hotel and putting it back on before going home.

Funny, I wore it while I slept with the clients and none of them had ever even noticed.

Or maybe it was that they hadn't cared.

Either way, thinking about it now, I definitely didn't need to be wearing it while I screwed someone else.

It just didn't seem right.

Some might say that I didn't love him because of what I was doing, but they would be wrong.

I loved him so much.

I was only at the hotel because of the contract, and that whole thing with Nolan had been a mistake.

I was emotional. We both were emotional.

But my mind was clear now, and I knew that Silas was everything that I'd never needed in a man.

And he was all mine.

As I moved around the lounge, Carmen followed me and spoke so negatively of Silas and told me that he couldn't be trusted and that I'd made the right decision by walking away from him before he hurt me even more.

I had to force myself not to roll my eyes at her and I was trying my best to bite my tongue.

She was such a hater!

But it was okay though.

This little bonding moment was just what I needed.

I needed her to learn to trust me and I was going to use Silas and say whatever else to make sure that she did.

After talking a little more, I headed to shower and she headed to do whatever it was that she did while everyone else on the floor were *serving* sex.

As I showered, I couldn't help but think about my life and this crazy situation that I was in.

I thought about how I'd ended up here; which in turn caused me to think about the baby.

It had been two weeks since I'd seen him and I missed him so much.

Nolan still wouldn't answer or return any of my phone calls. I couldn't believe that he had done something so foul.

And it was all to hurt me.

It was all because I couldn't give him the type of relationship that he wanted from me but on the flip side, neither could he.

He was married!

Not that his marriages ever really stopped him from doing what he wanted to do anyway.

I hated the fact that I didn't know where he lived.

He'd always offered to just pick the baby up.

Silas had taken me to see a lawyer and though he'd said that I could try to battle Nolan in court for rights and custody, at the end of the day, Nolan was the baby's biological father and pretty much everything was on his side of the fence.

But Silas said that he would continue to talk to a few of his friends and see what else he could do.

Nolan was a piece of work and I'd almost let him fool me into thinking otherwise.

And I was sure that his stupid ass cousin, Marie, had something to do with his crazy decision to keep the baby. I mean, why was she in the car with him in the first place that day?

She'd never been with him before.

She'd probably come along for the ride, just to see the look of pain on my face.

I could tell from that day on the bus that she was still bitter about what Keymar had done to her.

There was no telling what type of negativity she was putting in his ear.

It was clear that she had some sort of animosity towards me but I wasn't the one who had left her barefooted and pregnant.

That was Keymar…not me.

So, I couldn't be held responsible for a dead man's mistakes.

But she wasn't even an issue at this point.

At the end of the day, I just wanted the baby back.

And I was willing to do anything.

Finally freshened up, I headed to *my room* with everything, but sex, on my mind.

I opened the door to find two men inside.

Confused, I stepped back out of the room to look at Carmen as she walked a new maid to the room next to mine.

"Oh, yeah, I forgot to tell you that you were booked for a threesome. Enjoy," she said with a smirk on her face as she entered the room with the timid woman behind her.

Oh how I hated her!

I peeked back into my room and both men were naked and ready to go.

I'd never had a threesome, considering that I'd backed out of the one with Keymar.

To be honest, I was definitely feeling some kind of way.

The memories of what he'd done to me, taunted me for a second, but I knew that in this situation, I didn't have a choice.

This was absurd but this was the game and for the moment, Carmen was still in charge.

The sooner I got started, the sooner it would be over, I thought as I closed the door behind me, and as a single tear rolled down my face.

Arriving home later that day, I was happy to see Silas and Horizon.

Silas had definitely stepped into the role of being a father figure for her and I was truly thankful.

The way that she interacted with him made me feel as though I had deprived her of something for the first three years of her life and I felt bad.

Sure it wasn't our fault that Keymar had passed away, but it was me who refused to get back into the dating world all of that time.

But love came right when it was supposed to.

Horizon was standing on a chair beside Silas, as he chopped cucumbers for a salad.

"Hi baby," he said.

I kissed them both and then sat in one of the kitchen chairs.

Silas wanted us to move to his place.

His home was three times the size of mine, but it didn't have the same sentimental value.

It didn't have the same southern charm.

So, he was staying with us and said that if it meant that much to me that we could settle there forever and he would put his place on the market.

He would do anything to make me happy.

"How was work?" Silas asked.

"It was fine I guess," I said.

"You know you don't have to work right?"

"I know. It won't be much longer."

"So, when were you going to tell me that you worked for Carmen?"

At his comment, I almost pissed on myself, literally.

What?

What did he mean?

How did he know?

Carmen told him didn't she?

That b....

"I put two and two together that night. It was clear that she's your boss and that you are a maid at the hotel that she runs. I guess I understand why you wanted to hide that you were a maid; it isn't the best job. Really, I do understand. But now I'm telling you that you don't have to clean up after people anymore. I can take care of you. You know that. You don't have to be anyone's maid," Silas said, interrupting my last thought.

I let out a deep breath.

Okay, so he didn't know the whole truth.

He just thought that I was a maid.

I could deal with that.

"I'm sorry for saying that I ran a hotel instead of just being honest. At the time, I guess I didn't know how," I said.

"It's fine. I guess that makes us even. But let's make a deal---no more secrets and lies okay?"

I smiled at him and nodded.

"Okay."

Of course I didn't actually mean it, at least not yet.

But soon enough I would be free from the hotel and I would have a clean slate.

And I was going to be Mrs. Okeke and I couldn't wait!

"Oh, and I wanted to ask you something," Silas said.

For some reason, I got nervous.

I thought that maybe it was going to be something hotel related that maybe he found or something, but it wasn't.

"I was wondering if I would be able to adopt Horizon. Once we are married of course. And give her *our* last name," Silas said.

Aww!

I just loved him!

He was so sweet and he loved us so much.

A few tears fell from my eyes and unable to speak, I just shook my head.

Silas smiled and so did Horizon as if she knew what we were talking about.

This was all I'd ever wanted and now I had it.

The only thing missing was the baby…

***

"So, he hasn't called or anything?" Josephine asked.

We were having one of our monthly sister dates.

Sonni hadn't been able to attend this one, but she promised to be at the next one.

"No. I haven't heard from him. And I miss the baby so much," I said to her.

We were having lunch at a crowded restaurant and though I wanted to become emotional, there were too many people around for all of that.

If he would just let me see him, maybe that would do for the time being.

That was all that I asked.

I just wanted to see him, but Nolan was ignoring me.

I still hadn't heard one single word from him since that day.

Josephine and I talked a little more about the situation and then soon changed the subject.

Josephine had such an amazing sense of humor and I was actually able to enjoy a few laughs.

She could have been a comedian as funny as she was.

She was a stay at home mom, just like I used to be.

Her husband Grant brought home all the money and all she had to do was take care of him and the kids.

To me, that was how it was supposed to be.

To me, that life was perfect.

Josephine abruptly stopped talking.

"Envy," he said

I turned around to put a face with the voice.

Oh no…it was Mr. Ben from the hotel.

Immediately I felt nervous because I knew that recently he had been acting crazy and I was unsure of what he might do or say.

Not to mention that I had never seen any man outside of the hotel that I had entertained, so I just didn't know what to expect.

I just knew that there was about to be trouble.

"I just wanted to say hello…and that I love you," he said.

I looked at him like the fool that he was.

Strangely, he smiled.

Psycho!

"Oh, and here you go. This should take care of your lunch, both of yours and the tip. You know I always leave a *tip*," he said, laying a hundred dollar bill on the table.

Without another word, and with a wink, he walked away.

That crazy bastard!

And did he say that he loved me?

He didn't love me!

Sex is not love…sex is just sex!

Before I could even turn back around to face Josephine, I spotted another fellow headed in my direction.

Damn it, I'm never eating at this restaurant again!

But wait a minute this run-in could be a good thing.

"I just wanted to say thank you for everything. It's because of you that I had the strength to leave his cheating ass! I'm divorcing his sorry ass and I'm moving on with my life honey! We're already separated and he's gone. I don't know where he is and I don't care. Who knows, one day I might pay you another visit at the hotel, and maybe this time you can give me that sample that you owe me. Enjoy your lunch," he said, waved and then walked away.

It wasn't until he walked off that I actually breathed.

And I noticed that he was a lot more feminine than he had been at the hotel.

I guess he'd felt the need to blend in.

I had no idea as to what he was going to say, but the one thing that I was going to ask him, he'd said it.

He and Nolan were over and he didn't know where Nolan was.

So where the hell was he?

I tried to become settled back at the table but I could feel Josephine staring at me.

"Who were those men?" Josephine asked.

Oh hell.

"Just some guys that I know."

"You mean some guy you slept with, the first one, especially since he says that he loves you. And what did the second one mean about a husband, the hotel and a *sample*?"

I just looked at her.

"I know you hear me talking to you," she said.

"Josephine, it's nothing. Just let it go," I said to her.

She rolled her eyes and changed the subject.

"So, when is the wedding?"

"I'm not sure yet. But it will be soon," I responded to her and took a bite of my food.

"Do you really think that Silas is the one?"

Her question surprised me.

Did I think that Silas was the one?

If there was such a thing…he had to be.

We got along great and I could honestly say that I could see myself spending the rest of my life with him.

"Yes. Yes he's the one," I said.

"Just make sure that you're sure. You wouldn't want to marry the wrong one," she said.

I looked at her.

"What do you mean by that Josephine?"

She took a sip of her drink.

"I should have married Mark."

I stared at her.

Mark was our sister, Sonni's, husband.

Though Josephine had made a remark about the two of them having an affair at Horizon's birthday party, we hadn't discussed it.

"I knew him first Envy. Way before he'd met Sonni. I'd had an affair on Grant in the early years of our marriage. He was always so busy, and at the time I didn't have kids, so I was lonely. So, I met Mark and we had a thing. I broke it off with Mark once I got pregnant because I wasn't for sure whose baby it was. Hell, to this day, I still don't know but I knew then that I was playing with fire and if I didn't end things right then, things were going to get messy," Josephine said.

Oh my, here we go.

"We didn't see each other for a while and the next time I saw him was when he was being introduced to us by Sonni, as her fiancé. You know how private she is, so he hadn't known at first that we were sisters. Mark and I had a brief conversation and he'd expressed that he didn't know but he'd also said that what we had was nothing and that he was still going to marry Sonni. For years, nothing ever happened between us and then once we bought the house a little closer to them, things started to get tricky. We started to run into each other here and there and somehow we just started at it again. We both know that it's wrong and that we need to tell our spouses the truth. Or at least leave them, but it never seems like the right time. Why do you think I've gained so much weight? I'm miserable in my marriage. I'm tired of pretending and living a lie. So, I eat to deal with it. But the truth is that I'm in love with my sister's husband and no matter how hard I try, I just can't help it. And I feel so bad about it. Grant is so good to me and the kids. He doesn't deserve this, but I can't help the way that I feel," Josephine concluded.

I couldn't believe my ears!

They sure don't make *sisters* the way that they used to do they?

I couldn't imagine being in that situation.

I mean the situation with Nolan hadn't exactly been right, but at least he hadn't been married to Tia and at least Tia was dead.

Harshly put, but it definitely made all the difference.

And I hadn't been in love with him either.

But what Josephine was going through had to be Hell on earth for her.

I didn't know what to say or even where to start.

But I knew one thing was for sure and that was that if she didn't end it, eventually something bad was going to become of it.

Sonni was already a little different; and I wasn't sure if her different included crazy or not, but all I could see was disaster up ahead.

We finished the rest of our lunch pretty much in silence.

After all, what was there left to say?

We stood up to leave and I gave the waitress the entire hundred dollar bill that Mr. Ben had left behind.

The waitress smiled.

There was nothing like a big tip…and I could testify to that.

***

"You wanna grab lunch?" Carmen asked.

She had been all over me since I'd told her that Silas and I were no longer together.

I was still mad about the threesome thing, but I had work to do, so I had to get over it.

Carmen was still a bitch, majority of the time, but I could tell that she was trying to tone it down so that she could be nosey.

She was always asking about Silas.

And I do mean, always.

She wanted to know if we were speaking again and the details as to what he'd done.

She would often say that she hated him, but despite what he'd done to her, I found her words hard to believe.

I could tell that she wanted me to feel the hatred towards him *too*, but I didn't.

I absolutely loved him!

Since I was just a little over a month from leaving the hotel, I'd finally set a wedding date!

It was currently the beginning of August, and the wedding date was set for next April on the 12th.

My contract would expire near the end of September due to taking the month off after Tia's death, and after that, wedding plans were going to be in full effect!

Silas was the man, and he was my man.

Lucky, lucky me!

I couldn't wait to spend the rest of my life with him.

But Carmen didn't need to know all that.

Detective Wiley was calling almost daily for new information but each time I had nothing new to tell him.

He made it clear that if I couldn't do the job that he would find someone that could and he constantly reminded me that I would go down with everyone else.

Even if the walls didn't come tumbling down until after my contract was up and I was already gone, he assured me that I would still be held accountable for the things that I'd done while there; unless I got him what he needed it.

I wasn't sure if he was trying to scare the crap out of me or what, but I needed to check more into the charges.

I mean of course prostitution was illegal in North Carolina, but it wasn't a major offense. I was sure that somehow tax evasion and maybe even money laundry was probably tied into what we were doing here.

Who knows what other charges he could or would try to slap us with; and that was just the maids.

I'm sure Carmen and the others would be hit with all kinds of things.

So, basically, I couldn't take his threats lightly.

It was time to get down and dirty and find what *we* needed, so, I agreed to go to lunch with Carmen.

I was praying that I would make it through it without trying to stab her with a fork.

While waiting for our food, Silas called a few times and Carmen always glanced in my direction as if she was trying to catch a peek at my phone.

I finally turned it on silent and put it in my purse.

"So, what happens when I leave next month?" I asked her, hoping to get on the subject of the hotel.

"What do you mean? You go on with your life. There have been hundreds of women that have come through the hotel and participated in the *activities* of the thirteenth floor and once they left, I never saw them again. No one has ever come back again," Carmen said.

I listened to every word that she said attentively.

She must have been doing this for a very long time.

"Carmen, were you ever one of us?" I asked her.

She looked at me and then started to laugh.

"Honey no. I could never do what you do. I would never sale my body. I have too much class to be some *paid whore*. If anyone was getting some of this, it was because I wanted them to have it. Not because they'd paid for it."

What?

I promise, more than the Devil wanted souls, I wanted to smack the hell out of her!

All of the pep-talks and pushing the fantasy of what comes with the thirteenth floor and she'd never even experienced it?

Bitch!

"So, you have just been the overseer…the entire time?" I asked hoping that she would answer.

"Since the very beginning."

I could tell that she'd wished that she could take the words back as soon as she'd said them.

I was getting too personal, so hurriedly I changed the subject and pretended to *like* her for the rest of our lunch.

As soon as my day at the hotel was over, I called the detective just to give him that small bit of information.

It wasn't a lot.

But it was an idea of the timeframe.

Carmen was only about forty, if that, maybe late thirties, so I was sure that it all may have started ten to fifteen years ago.

Maybe they could go back to where she worked before then or find her hired date for the hotel.

That part wasn't my job, but I was hoping that it would soon be over.

I was just ready for it all to be over.

Thinking about the hotel and why I'd started doing what I was doing in the first place, made me think about Tia.

I missed her so much.

With the baby gone, I didn't feel as close to her as I had before.

I felt as though I was losing her.

I felt as though the baby kept her presence near but I didn't feel it anymore.

I felt as though I'd failed her in some way.

With her on my mind, I decided to stop and get some flowers and to go visit her grave.

This would be my first time going there since the funeral and before I'd even arrived, I started to cry.

It was still hard to believe that she was gone.

I walked slowly through the cemetery as I tried to get my thoughts together.

I guess I just imagined my life differently.

And I imagined Tia's going different as well.

She was supposed to have a business degree and working the job of her dreams by now.

But instead she was somewhere in Heaven; worry and stress free.

Maybe she was the lucky one.

Still thinking of her, as I neared her grave, someone was already there visiting her…

Nolan!

At the sight of me, immediately he looked uncomfortable and maybe even afraid.

Suddenly I didn't feel sad anymore.

I felt angry!

I walked directly into his personal space.

"Where is the baby?" I asked him furiously.

Before I could stop myself, I hit him with the flowers in my hand that were supposed to be for my sister's grave.

Nolan just stood there at first and finally he tried to restrain me.

"Where is he? I miss him so much. Why would you do that? Why would you take him from me?" I whined.

I knew better than to cross the line with him in the first place but believe me if I had known that he was capable of doing something so cruel, I definitely would have ran for the nearest exit when things started to heat up between us.

I guess that's what I get for thinking with my hormones, instead of my head.

That damn hotel has ruined me!

Nolan was being strangely quiet and no matter what I said or how many times I tried to swing on him, he wasn't saying a word.

He just stared at me as though I was crazy or something.

He stared at me as though he didn't even know me.

After a few more minutes of listening to me scream at him, finally he let go of my arms and opened his mouth.

"I'm sorry Envy, it was his idea. I'm just sorry," he said and turned to walk away.

Really?

It had been *his* idea?

Who was he talking about?

His husband?

So, he'd told him about confronting me after all and then convinced Nolan to take the baby from me?

Who does that to somebody?

And wait a minute, I'd just seen him, and he'd said that they were getting a divorce.

So either he was lying about not knowing where Nolan was, or things went sour after he thought that he was going to have the perfect little family.

That bastard!

Nolan was getting further and further away, so I called after him.

"Nolan please. Please just let me see him. You can have him. Just let me see him. He's all I have left of her. I'll come to you or whatever you want me to do. I just want to see him and hold him. I miss his big brown eyes and that sweet, cute smile. Please. Can I go with you to see him?" I cried.

I guess my tears pulled at the strings of his heart because he stopped walking and turned to face me.

He stared at me and I could see the sympathy that he had for me all over his face.

I was getting through to him.

He was finally giving in.

"Nolan please, I'm begging you. Please just let me see him," I said again.

Nolan looked at me a while longer and then he did something strange.

He nodded his head behind me.

Confused, I turned around to face Tia's grave and…

Right beside hers was a small tombstone that read:

In Memory of my Precious baby boy: Nolan F. Jackson Jr.

What?

***

I'd been sick for days.

Not physically; but mentally and emotionally.

Words couldn't describe the way that I felt.

As the story goes, the baby had passed away the week before from Sudden Infant Death syndrome.

Nolan had gone to wake the baby up that evening to feed him and he'd already made his journey back to Heaven to join his mother.

The whole thing gave me flashbacks of finding Keymar, dead, beside me the morning that he'd passed away.

It hit home for me, hard, and since finding out the news, nothing in my life seemed to make sense.

The saddest part of all was that Nolan hadn't even called to tell us about the baby's death.

He'd had a whole memorial for the baby and hadn't called to say one, single word.

Had I not seen him that day at the cemetery, I would have never even known.

Well, I guess burying the baby beside his mother was his way of hoping that one day I would actually see it and pay attention to it.

It was his weak ass attempt of ensuring that I found out but he was dead wrong.

How could you do that to somebody?

He'd hit way below the belt and if I could kill him and get away with it, he would have been a dead man by now.

The day at the cemetery, after making sure that I saw the baby's name, I fell to my knees in tears, and Nolan simply walked away.

He'd waited until he was gone to call and leave the details of the baby's death on my voicemail.

Do you know how heartless a person has to be to do something like that?

By the time I'd tried to call Nolan back for more details and to curse his ass out, he'd already disconnected his number.

He was just as crazy as his dead wife had been and in a way.

He was pure evil.

But the after effect of the news was what was really weighing me down.

I was so heartbroken that I could barely move.

I wasn't sleeping.

I wasn't eating.

I wasn't even going in to "work" at the hotel.

I just couldn't believe that the baby was dead.

And I couldn't believe that I'd missed his last days. I couldn't help but think that maybe he would have still been alive if he had been home with me.

You just never know.

But the thought of it hurt me even more.

"What can I do?" Silas asked.

"Nothing."

"You have to eat. You have to pull yourself together. Horizon misses you. I miss you," Silas said.

I heard him and though my heart wanted to respond to him, I couldn't.

I just didn't know what to say.

After waiting for me to respond and getting nothing, Silas excused himself from the room.

A few minutes later I heard the front door slam.

I was sure that he was getting frustrated but he had to understand.

No matter how much I tried I just couldn't seem to shake away the thoughts and the pain.

But I knew that I was going to have to snap out of it all sooner or later.

At the end of the day I still had obligations and a daughter of my own that needed me.

Since the news, I hadn't really spoken to anyone.

Everyone called to check on me, but I never bothered to answer.

But hopefully soon I would get myself together.

I forced myself to send Silas a text message.

He had to be damn tired of all of the things that had gone on in my life since he'd been in the picture but had it not been for him, I don't think that I would have made it through.

I waited for him to text me back and when he didn't, I headed to the front porch to get some fresh air.

I sat in silence as I watched my neighbors that lived in the house that used to be Rodney's and his wife's.

The wife waved in my direction and I forced myself to smile at her.

It was her, her husband, and they had five kids.

They kept to themselves most of the time, but every time I saw them load into their up to date mini-van, secretly I envied them.

I couldn't wait to be them and I knew that with Silas a life like theirs wasn't too far away.

I lived for family time and activities together, just like we used to do when I was a child.

There were so many memorable moments from my childhood, mostly good, and I just wanted Horizon to have what I had; fun, siblings, and loving parents.

Sure my parents had problems, issues and maybe even a few secrets but there was no doubt in my mind that they didn't have a piece of true love.

And that was all I'd ever wanted for myself.

I just wanted a piece of it.

With love on my mind, I headed back into the house to check my phone to see if Silas had texted back.

As soon as I entered the bedroom, my phone started to ring.

I glanced at it and saw that it was the detective.

I'd been ignoring all of his calls too, so I was sure that he was frustrated with me as well.

I ignored the call and read Silas's text message instead.

I couldn't help but smile.

Never had I felt so much love.

Silas's love was strong, full, and it kept me wanting more.

After the detective called another ten times, I figured that I had better answer it.

"We need you at the hotel…now! Some of our guys are watching it, of course, and they just spotted a man in a limo covered from head to toe going into the hotel. He had on a hat, sunglasses and even a scarf. It's the summertime, so if that's not suspicious, I don't know what is. They couldn't see his face, so we need to see if you can get a look at him."

I frowned knowing that I really didn't have a choice and knowing that he was probably too late with his request.

Most of the time, I didn't see other clients, unless one was going into a room while I was coming out of mine, or the other way around.

We never went to their sleeping quarters if they were staying over at the hotel; it was forbidden and even written in the contract.

There were a few times that I'd caught a glimpse of a few, but there were so many faces of the thirteenth floor that I only had room in my head to at least attempt to remember the faces of my regulars; just because tips were involved.

There had to be hundreds of men that came to the hotel for *extra-curricular* activities, on a weekly basis.

Though when I'd started, I'd assumed that it was only a few girls on the top floor, I'd later found out that there were about fifty, and we were constantly getting new "maids".

That's a whole lot of booty being sold in one place.

One different shifts and different days; still yet it was a lot.

But though I was mourning, I couldn't go to jail behind my sorrows, so I forced myself to get dressed and in less than half an hour, I was arriving at the hotel.

Obviously, the informants were watching me because as soon as I parked, my phone ranged again.

"You missed him," the detective said and hung up in my face.

How rude!

Police or not, he could get cursed out too!

Who the hell does he think that he is?

I was extremely aggravated, so I sat there for just a second and took a deep breath.

Envy, if you don't get it together, you are going to go to jail.

I knew that I didn't have a choice but to cooperate, but I didn't want to.

I was going to have to get over the baby situation and keep going.

Life surely didn't stop and if I didn't get myself together Tia and the baby wouldn't be the only ones that I lost.

****

Chapter FOUR

"Um, I've missed you so much," one of my clients said as he finished his business on top of me.

He was usually one that I somewhat enjoyed but though my body was in the room, my head was somewhere else.

Surprisingly, I was thinking about moving far away.

Though I'd always wanted to raise my family in my parent's house, I suddenly had a change of heart.

The house held too many memories, especially of Tia and the baby and it was time for me to let it go.

Of course I'd paid the bank back every penny that was owed to them, but it was time for me move on.

Though Silas had placed his house on the market already, I figured that we could go looking for a new home together.

As for my parent's house, I was going to offer it to one of my sister's and their families, which I was sure they would decline, and once they did, I was simply going to keep it as a family home.

You never know what the future holds, and who might actually need it.

After my client was dressed and my tip was in my hand, I hurriedly cleaned up my room and since he was my last client of the day, I rushed to shower so that I could go home.

Carmen had been somewhat avoiding me for the last few days.

She'd given me the hardest time about laying out of work behind finding out about the death of the baby but since I'd been back she had been fairly distant.

But the days were still counting down so I had to get busy.

The detective had made it clear that if I didn't have what I needed by the end of my contract that I wouldn't be able to just walk away.

Whatever!

When my contract was up, I was getting the hell away from this hotel, and nothing and nobody was going to stop me.

So, I had to get on it and stay on it.

As far as I knew, Carmen still didn't have a clue that Silas and I were still engaged, so I figured that her distance was due to her own personal issues.

I looked for her on my way out but I didn't see her in her top office, so I headed down the elevator.

Entering her downstairs office, she wasn't there either so I headed towards the door.

I could get my money from her tomorrow.

But suddenly, I stopped dead in my tracks.

I turned around to face her file cabinet.

If memory served me correctly, she'd gotten my key and my sign-on bonus money out of it, so obviously she utilized it just as much as she utilized the one upstairs.

There had to be something in there that I could use.

I inched towards it but decided that maybe I should wait.

I turned back towards the door to find Carmen standing there.

She just stood there, looking at me.

I could tell that she wasn't herself.

She looked stressed out or maybe she looked depressed.

Whatever she was, she wasn't the million dollar image that I was used to seeing when it came to her.

"You need something? Well, other than this," she said, handing me one of the envelopes that were in her hands.

She definitely looked *off.*

"No, I turned around because I thought I left my phone upstairs, but I forgot that I put it in my bra," I patted my chest and Carmen quickly glanced at it.

"Oh."

Carmen walked towards her desk and sat down.

Something definitely wasn't right.

"Are you okay?" I asked her, with as much concern as I possibly could.

I still didn't like her, but the more I pretended to, the easier it became to keep my game face on.

"I'm fine Envy. Shut the door on your way out," she said and turned her chair towards the back wall.

She's such a lunatic!

She made it so hard for anyone to want to be in her presence.

Without shutting the door, I walked out of her office and out of the hotel.

It was hot and sticky and I couldn't get to my car fast enough.

"Envy," I turned around to see the detective behind me.

His face always made me frown.

If he would wear a mask, I might be tempted to lick him.

His body was teasingly seductive, but I didn't see how any woman would be able to get over his face.

He wasn't wearing a wedding ring so most likely other woman couldn't stomach the sight of him either.

Not to mention that he was an asshole.

"Anything new?" he asked.

I didn't understand why he felt the need to ask me damn near every day!

I knew what was at stake and I knew what I had to do.

When I got something new, I would call him, but he didn't get that.

"Not yet," I said and opened my car door.

"Well, we need something and we need it fast," he said, placed on his shades and walked away.

Inside my car, I had little time to think on the situation because Silas called before I could even pull off.

I'd had to apologize to him for how I had been acting lately.

I was sure that he felt neglected but hopefully I'd made it up to him the night before.

"Are you on your way home?" Silas asked.

"Of course, I can't wait to see your face," I said flirtatious.

Silas chuckled and I could tell that he probably had a big *Kool-Aid* smile plastered on his face.

He loved me so much and I couldn't wait to give him all of me.

That's why I had to find what the cops needed.

I had to hurry up and get away from the hotel.

I arrived home only minutes later and before I got out the car, I sat there for a moment just to think.

The car was my favorite place to collect my thoughts; I'd gotten that from Mama.

Mama would arrive home, but she would sit in her car for maybe an hour or so, every day, before she would come into the house.

I would often ask her why she did it and she would always say that every day a person needed quiet and alone time.

She'd said it was just as important to the mind as sleep was to the body, and I would be the first to say that I agreed.

I sat there and thought about everything that was going on around me.

I even managed to think about the future but for some reason I wasn't as sure about it as I had been before.

Things could change in a flash and it wasn't always in a good way.

To be honest, I was scared to death.

What happens if I couldn't find what the detective needed?

What happens if I ended up going to jail with everyone else?

I just couldn't let that happen to me.

But as shady as Carmen was, there was no way of knowing if I was ever going to get anything out of her.

So then what?

Who would look after Horizon if I went to prison?

Maybe Silas and I should start the adoption process before we got married.

But would he even want her if I went down for being some hotel whore?

What would happen to us?

There was just so much that I had to lose and I just couldn't afford to.

I had to make Carmen trust me.

I had to give her the friend that I was sure that she'd never had and probably always wanted.

Feeling overwhelmed but knowing that I couldn't show it, I pulled myself together and headed into the house.

I smiled once I opened the door to see that candlelight and rose petals were everywhere.

What is Silas up to?

I woke up the next morning feeling great.

The night before had been nothing less than amazing!

Silas had managed to get Horizon to my sister, cook dinner, give me a full body massage, and sex me speechless.

I would kill somebody over him, I swear I would.

I looked over at him.

He was still asleep.

I wished that I could just lie in bed with him all day and do nothing but I knew that I couldn't.

The hotel was where I *had* to be.

At the sound of vibrating, I looked at the table beside my bed at my phone, but it wasn't mine.

Glancing over Silas's sleeping mass, to the table on his side, I saw that it was his.

His phone ranged all day and night and he was always on his laptop.

I only knew that he had his hands in the stock market, so I was sure that required being available by phone or email often, so I never complained.

Silas's phone stopped vibrating and immediately it started up again.

Quietly I got out of bed and tip-toed to his side.

Silas moved a little so I stood still and once he started to snore again, I reached for his phone.

As soon as I grabbed it, the vibrating stopped, but immediately it started back again.

My eyes widened as I saw who was calling.

Out of instinct, I frowned.

Why in the hell was Carmen calling his phone?

**

I hated the fact that I couldn't ask Carmen why she'd called Silas.

I had to bite my tongue because I couldn't let her know that he and I were still involved.

It just ate me up in the inside.

Why in the hell was she calling him?

Were they still involved?

Why did she even have his number?

They hadn't been married in years, surely his number had been changed since then, so why, what, when and how was it that she had it or had the need to call him?

I had so many questions and not enough answers.

I was planning to ask Silas but it hadn't exactly been the right time.

Oh, but believe me, I was going to.

I assumed that Carmen was in a better mood than she had been in last week because she was just talking away.

Of course I had to pretend to be interested because I had to stay on her good side.

"So, since we're both single, let's go out and do something tonight," she said.

I wanted to scream, HELL NO right in her face, but I knew that this may be an opportunity to get information out of her.

"Okay," I said nonchalantly.

I already knew that it was going to be a long night.

And I definitely wasn't looking forward to it.

"Where are you going?" Silas asked later on that evening after dinner.

"Oh, some girls from work wanted to get together and have a few drinks. I hope you don't mind," I said to Silas as he wrapped his arms around my waist.

He kissed my neck.

Usually, my juices would have begun to flow, but he was on my bad side until I found out the truth behind Carmen's calls.

"No, I don't mind. Horizon and I can watch a movie until she falls asleep," he said, still loving all over me.

I was trying my best to hold my tongue but it was killing me not to say anything.

So finally, I let it out.

"Why was Carmen calling your phone?" I asked him.

Silas stopped kissing me and looked at me.

He didn't hesitate too long.

"She calls me all the time. I never answer though," he said.

"How does she even know your number?"

"She got it when I called to tell her about the passing of my ex-wife, and daughter; her sister and niece. I'd gotten hers from one of her other siblings. She'd actually hung up on me that day; which is why I'd gone by the hotel that time to speak to her. But for a while now, she just calls, especially after the whole proposal," he said.

Well, it sounded like the truth.

So, now the issue was why was Carmen continuing to call and bother him?

She couldn't possibly still want him...could she?

There was no telling when it came to Carmen.

But I would never know because for the moment I couldn't say a word to her about it.

Damn!

"Okay," I said to Silas and continued to get ready.

A few minutes later, I was out the door, heading to meet the Devil's mistress…Carmen.

Seeing Carmen, I looked and felt as though I was her real life maid standing next to her.

I'd dressed to impress, at least I'd thought that I had, but I didn't compare to Carmen.

She was *snatched*, stunning, from head to toe.

Her tight fit red dress hugged each and every one of her small curves, just right, and she had diamonds everywhere: her neck, her ears, her wrists, her shoes and even on her bra that was peeking out of the top part of her dress.

I definitely needed to go shopping.

I had more than enough money, and not to mention that Silas had even more and he didn't mind sharing it, but I guess I was so used to hiding it and where it came from that I hardly ever splurged.

But if I was going to try to hang around Carmen, I was going to have to.

But even though she was dressed like a movie star, my hips and curves were still getting all of the attention and I could tell that it bothered her.

So I guess we were even.

We headed to the bar and I was surprised that Carmen had chosen a place that wasn't all that classy.

I was surprised at how laid back it was.

It wasn't a club; but there was music and a few people in their own world swaying back and forth to the beat.

Hearing Carmen order three different drinks, at one time, I assumed that she just wanted to let her hair down.

And that's exactly what she did.

I had a few drinks but Carmen had so many that I'd lost count.

After only two hours of being there, Carmen was as drunk as a skunk and she walked around the place either making sexual advances or inappropriately touching every man in sight.

She was so drunk that she'd started to call me Nicole.

Nicole was her deceased sister and Silas's deceased wife.

I was surprised that she was on her mind as much as she hated her, but for the rest of the night, that was what she called me and every single time I answered.

I guess in a weird way I thought that it might make her spill her guts a lot faster.

I don't know, but my gut told me to go with the flow.

She told me, "Nicole" that she missed me and she asked me why I'd gone after her husband, instead of finding my own.

She told me how much I hurt her and that she never forgave *me*.

I guess these were all of the things that she'd wanted to tell her real sister but she'd never gotten the chance to.

It's been said that a drunken man tells no tales, so I believed every word that came out of her mouth.

I allowed her to be drunk and act like a crazy person for as long as I could stand to watch her.

She was actually hilarious while she was drunk and I found myself smiling at her even when I didn't want to.

She made jokes and held on to my arm.

She was definitely likable at the moment and it was such a shame that she couldn't be this way while she was sober.

After a while, I led her out the door to my car.

I made sure that her car was locked and informed the valet that I was going to have to leave it and drive her home.

Once she threw up, I secured her in my car and we drove off.

I reached in her clutch to get her address from her license.

What?

Maybe I'd had a little too much to drink, so I closed my eyes for a second, opened them, and looked at her license again.

Even though she used her maiden name at work, her license still said Silas's last name.

Huh?

And the license had been renewed only a few years ago, so obviously she'd kept his last name.

But why on earth would she do that?

If my ex-husband had married my sister, and if for some odd reason I hadn't killed them both, there would be no way in hell that I would want any attachments or anything linking me to or reminding me of him.

Maybe she really was obsessed with him.

I shook my head and turned up the radio to try to keep myself from getting too upset and to drown out the sound of Carmen's weird moans.

We drove for quite some time.

When I saw that her house was located in Ballantyne, it became crystal clear to me that this woman had a hell of a lot of money.

Whatever she'd made over the years for bringing women *on* at the hotel had to be more than most people would ever see in their life time.

I had plenty of money in just a year's time, so I could only imagine what Carmen had stashed away.

Finally, I pulled up at a house with a gate.

The house was so big that I had to blink twice to make sure that I wasn't dreaming.

I was in complete awe.

What in the hell did one person need with all of this house?

"Carmen, I need the code to the gate," I asked her about three times.

She looked at me and laughed.

She made smart remarks and still called me her sister's name but finally she gave me what I needed to know.

"1115," she said and she appeared to have passed out.

As soon as she'd said it, one thought popped into my head.

I couldn't help but become frustrated.

1115…was Silas's birthday month and day.

At that moment, I was convinced that she really needed help.

It was obvious that she was still had a thing for Silas and was probably even still madly in love with him.

And not to mention her behavior at the hotel until I'd lied about our relationship.

But she was going to have to get over it because she couldn't have him.

He chose me…damn!

So get over it already lady!

Shaking my head, I drove up the driveway in admiration.

The beauty of the house couldn't be put into words.

I was in awe of the cars that I'd never even seen her drive.

I was even in awe of the fabulous, nothing less than perfect, landscape.

It was truly a sight to see.

As I'd always said, it just didn't make sense to have all of this and no one to come home to every night and share it with.

To be honest, despite the fact that I'd taken the position on the thirteenth floor for money purposes, I would have been just fine with an average job, an average man and love and happiness.

Stability, security and love were all of the things that a woman ever really needed.

I would take that life on any given day rather than to be rich and lonely.

I really would.

I left Carmen in the car and ranged the doorbell.

Surely she had to have a *real* maid or a butler or something, but no one came to the door.

So, I headed to the car and found her clutch again.

After trying what seemed like twenty or so different keys, finally I found one that actually fit.

I was eager to get inside for some reason but I entered the house with caution, and I was immediately swept off of my feet.

I was mesmerized at first sight.

The inside of Carmen's house was just as beautiful as the outside.

It was the house of every woman's dreams.

Hell, it was the house of my dreams.

I just couldn't believe that Carmen was actually living like this…but then again, yes I could.

She'd clearly been at the hotel for a long time and I was sure that she had one hell of a "salary" if that was what you wanted to call it for supplying *us* to the clients of the thirteenth floor.

Thinking of the hotel, I took the keys out of the front door.

I glanced back at Carmen who was still passed out in my car.

She wasn't waking up anytime soon.

This was the perfect time to find something, anything that might help the case that was being built against her, the hotel and everyone else.

I shut the front door, locked it, and placed her keys in my bra.

Now the question was, where do I start?

I walked all over the bottom half of the house.

It was decorated to perfection and it reminded me of a high priced doll house.

I was surprised that I didn't see pictures or a shrine dedicated to Silas, but thank goodness that I didn't.

Everything was tasteful and elegant.

Everything was an exact refection of Carmen if I must say so myself.

There were even a few pieces that had a little *bitch* to them; yep, Carmen had definitely designed every inch of this place.

Finally, I headed up the stairs.

I had to go into all of ten bedrooms until I finally found the one that looked to be Carmen's.

It looked more *lived* in than the other's and it had a closet full of everything that a girl could ever want.

I wanted to save the closet for last, so I headed to her dresser.

She had so many diamonds and pearls, fragrances, make-up that hadn't even gone to stores yet, and so much more.

This woman truly had it all.

Well, except the one thing that she wanted most.

Love.

I opened one of the smaller drawers and found a single, old, wedding photo of her and Silas.

They kind of looked happy…kind of.

Okay, so I was starting to feel just a little bad for her.

I knew what it was like to love someone with everything that you had in you, only to find out that they weren't who you thought they were.

But even if I left him, for real, he wouldn't want her.

He'd had plenty of years to go back to her, but he hadn't, and from how he spoke of her, I was sure that he wouldn't.

So she was going to have to face the truth one of these days and finally accept it and move on.

Placing the photo back down, I looked through the papers that were there too, but I didn't see anything about the hotel.

Finally, I headed back to her closet.

I tried to remain focused and not become overwhelmed but there were a few things that I wanted to steal and take home with me.

I was sure that she wouldn't even notice that they were gone.

Nevertheless, I started to go through things, hoping to find something, but there was nothing there.

There was nothing there but clothes, furs, purses and shoes with price tags that looked like social security numbers.

It was as if everything in there was brand, spanking new.

What did she do, wear everything once and then throw it away and go buy more?

Figuring that it was time to get back to Carmen, I took one last glance at the goodies in her closet, checked to make sure that everything was in its rightful place on her dresser, just as it was before, and then I headed out of the bedroom.

I closed the door and damn near had a heart attack.

Carmen was standing there and she was completely, butt ass, naked; except for all of the diamonds.

Though she'd seen all of the ladies on the floor bare ass and all, I'd never seen her undressed.

She looked damn good for her age.

"There's always a spare," she said waving the key at me.

I hadn't even thought about that.

I wondered how long she'd been standing there.

Carmen burped and the smell of alcohol harassed the hairs in my nose, almost making me nauseous.

"Am I attractive?" Carmen asked.

What?

Oh heck no, we were not going down that road!

I saw the way that she looked at me at times, and though they were questionable, I always tried to ignore them.

But she didn't have a *meat wagon* hanging in between her legs, so she definitely wasn't my type.

I didn't answer her question so she didn't bother to ask me again.

Instead she turned the nob to her bedroom door and went inside.

She headed straight for the huge bed that sat on a platform that you had to get to by walking up three small steps.

Carmen was mumbling something so I inched closer to hear her.

Though her words were running together, I finally figured out what it was that she was saying.

"Everybody uses somebody. All of them use me but no one wants me. They want money. They want women. I do everything that they say, but they still don't see me. The women love that I bring them to the money. The men love that I bring them the women. The bosses love that I'm so good at what I do. But no one loves me..." Carmen said.

Huh?

What did she mean?

What or who was she talking about?

Who are *they*?

Who are the bosses?

After she passed out again, I closed her door, headed down the stairs, placed her keys on the hook beside the door and locked up.

Inside the car, I noticed that her clutch wasn't there so she must've taken it inside with her.

I sped off in a hurry so that I could use the drive home to think.

Who was she talking about?

I'd thought that she would only want Silas to love her but obviously there were other candidates that were possibilities…but who?

I couldn't figure it all out but I finally had something to tell the detective.

Though she hadn't said it exactly, she'd made it clear that there was a "they" at the top of the operation; which meant probably a couple of people were in charge.

Now we just had to figure out who "they" were.

***

"I was probably terrible the other night huh?" Carmen asked.

Terrible was an understatement.

She was a hot ass mess!

But in a weird way, I liked her more while she was drunk.

She wasn't so uptight or stuck up, even though she had been trying to give her pussycat to every man in sight, I liked how loose she was.

I was still a little disappointed that I didn't find out as much as I wanted to, but the detective said that what little I did get out of her was the start of something.

But I knew that it wasn't enough.

So, I had to create other opportunities, which meant that I had to spend more time with Carmen's psychotic ass.

It might not be so bad if each time she was drunk.

Also, I was more than disturbed by the fact that Carmen was still so obsessed with Silas.

It was safe to say that even though she tried to hide it and even though she acted as though she hated him, she was still madly in love with him, for some odd reason.

I mean the fact that he'd left her for her sister, married her and had a child with her, still hadn't been enough to make Carmen stop feeling whatever it was that she felt for him.

It was sad, and maybe even a little scary.

But the reality of it all was that she needed help and counseling and I wanted so badly to tell her *a* truth that she needed to hear.

But I knew that I couldn't.

I truly did feel kind of sorry for her but at the end of the day, no one could help her; except her.

But no matter what small amount of sympathy I felt for her, she still couldn't have Silas.

He was mine.

He was my good thing and I wasn't going to let him go.

Hopefully she would be going away, soon, for a very long time, so I was sure that she wouldn't be a problem in the near future.

But I hated the part where I had to keep my mouth shut about every little thing.

I listened to Carmen as I dressed in a cat woman outfit for my married client, Mr. Ben.

I definitely wanted to keep a distance from him since running into him at the restaurant, but as long as he *ordered* me, I didn't have a choice but to *serve* him.

Carmen was still talking and I could tell that she was becoming more and more comfortable with me but if only she knew that she was making a terrible mistake.

Yes, I felt somewhat uncomfortable at times about what I was doing, but I couldn't help that I was presented with the opportunity to have a way out.

If I didn't do it, someone else would.

At the end of the day, we all had to pay for the choices that we'd made.

I was already paying for mine, in so many other ways, and I guess behind bars was the way that she was going to have to pay for hers.

It was the only way.

She briefly discussed services and pricing and told me that after Mr. Ben, my curves had been *reserved.*

She asked if we could maybe hang out again sometime soon and at the nod of my head, we went our separate ways.

I entered Room 313 with hopeful thoughts that on our next outing I would get more information out of her.

But at the crack of my whip, Mr. Ben, who was lying on the bed smiled as big as the fictional Cheshire cat.

The sooner I got started, the sooner it'll all be over.

But surely my last day here just couldn't come fast enough.

I was happy that the client that had reserved me for the last part of my shift hadn't wanted to have sex at all.

He just wanted to talk.

For some reason, most of my clients loved chatting with me.

I always found it weird, personally, asking a whore for life coaching and martial advice, but hey, if it was going to keep me from sucking and everything else in between, I would talk until I was tongue tied and blue in the face.

After hours of talking, it was time for me to go and I couldn't wait to get out of that place.

Maybe it was just me, but I always felt like something bad was going to happen; other than the whole police bringing the "house" down of course.

I arrived home to see that both of my sisters were there.

Josephine and Sonni had definitely been around a lot more lately, and I liked it.

The news of the baby's death was just one more thing that had pushed us closer together.

I was enjoying our newfound relationship and I was hoping that it was a permanent situation.

"Hello doll," Josephine chimed from one of the rocking chairs on the front porch.

Sonni waved and smiled.

I took a seat in the empty chair and took a deep breath.

"So, what do I owe the pleasure of this visit," I asked them both.

"We just wanted to come down since we were both free today. You're just leaving the hotel I can see," Josephine said.

I didn't comment, out of fear that she would want to ask more questions about my day at the hotel.

I really wasn't in the mood to be interrogated.

"Are you still moving out of the house? I was wondering if the kids and I could have it," Josephine replied after seeing that I wasn't going to say anything.

Sonni and I both looked at her.

I guess we both caught on to the fact that she hadn't mentioned that her husband Grant was coming with them.

Grant was the definition of cool, calm, and collected. He was a man of a few words; the complete opposite of Josephine. She was always running off with her mouth, and he was really quiet. But we all knew that he really loved Josephine and that he would do anything in the world to keep her happy.

But obviously he wasn't doing enough.

They'd been together since their teen years as well and had married as soon as they were old enough to.

He had been around so long that he was like the brother that none of us ever had.

"Um, what about Grant?" I asked her.

Josephine turned her focus to the cars passing by.

But she knew that she didn't have a choice but to answer my question.

"We're getting a divorce," she said.

I guess it wasn't all that of a surprised to me, but I had to play my position.

"Why?"

"Oh, I can answer that question. It's because she's in love with *my* husband," Sonni said.

Aw, hell!

****

Chapter FIVE

Josephine and I both stared at Sonni, waiting to see what she would say next.

"Isn't that right Josephine? Aren't you in love with *my* husband? Aren't you having sex with *my* husband? I guess *sisters* aren't all they are made out to be huh?" Sonni asked and then giggled, just a little as if something was funny.

Josephine looked like a deer in headlights.

I knew that she didn't have the slightest idea as to what she was supposed to say, so she started to cry instead.

Sonni on the other hand, looked as though if she *blinked* twice, Josephine was going to croak over and die.

"Do you love my husband Josephine?" Sonni asked.

"Sonni maybe now isn't the time to---" I started to say but she cut me off.

"No, Envy, now is the perfect time," Sonni said pointing a finger in my direction.

I hushed, although I had a bad feeling that things were about to get out of hand.

I wondered where Horizon and Silas were finally noticing that his car wasn't in the driveway.

"Yes, I love him. I always have," Josephine admitted.

Damn...wrong answer.

Sonni looked at her for a few seconds as if she was trying to find the words to say or as though she was trying to keep herself from punching Josephine in the back of her head.

Either way, I was waiting for her words or actions, like old folks were waiting on the Rapture.

Finally, Sonni opened her mouth to take me out of my misery.

"Good. It's good that you love him…because I don't," she said.

Wait…

What?

I was definitely not expecting that!

What did she mean that she didn't *love* her husband?

Josephine stopped crying and looked at Sonni confused.

We both waited for her to explain.

"I've never loved him. I don't even think I love my kids…at least not like a mother should. I only married him because I didn't want to be alone. Everyone always had something to say about me being alone, or the fact that I was a loner and I guess I started to believe them and started to believe that something was wrong with me. So, I got married and had kids like a normal person, when the truth is…I'm not normal. I've never loved them, any of them. Not like most people love. Not like I should. I don't know why. I just don't," Sonni said.

I looked at her in disbelief.

To hear her say those words made me extremely heartbroken.

Sonni had always been weird as I said, but to say that she didn't love her husband or even her kids just didn't make sense to me.

Who wouldn't love their own kids?

"I can't explain why I feel the way that I do. It's just the way that I am. I don't even love you guys the way that I'm supposed to. Not like y'all probably love me. I think the only person that I have ever truly loved was Mama. Not Daddy…just Mama. I ask myself why, but I just don't know. I've known for years that I needed to see someone about it but I never did. I know that something wasn't right with me, but I never tried to get help. Maybe it's who I am. I don't know if it's a psychological thing, or a result of a repressed trauma. I just don't know. I just know that I have felt this way for as long as I can remember. So, Josephine, if you love him, you can have him…when I die," Sonni said.

I thought she was being sarcastic at first, but the look on her face told me that she wasn't.

"I have cancer," Sonni said and removed the wig from her head.

She was completely bald!

What?

No…she was going to die too?

I was sick and tired of people dying in my life.

Come on now!

"I've had it for a while and I don't have long left to live. So, I would appreciate it if I could have my husband, to myself, so that I don't have to face death alone. After I'm gone, he's all yours. Just make sure you take care of my kids too. Maybe you can love them in a way that I never could," Sonni said and placed her wig back on her head.

Josephine was crying so loud that I thought that the neighbors were going to come outside.

I was crying too, but of course Sonni wasn't.

She didn't look sad at all.

Something was really wrong with her, internally.

I'd always seen it.

I'd always known it.

But at this point it didn't matter whether she loved us back or not because we loved her even if she didn't love us; although Josephine had a funny way of showing it, with the whole sleeping with her husband and all.

Josephine made the first move and hugged Sonni and I followed.

Josephine and I cried as we hugged her.

Sonni just sat there for a while and finally she told us that everything was going to be okay.

My biggest regret was that I didn't show her that I loved her more. I just accepted her for the way that she was and hadn't tried to get through to her.

But I wished that I had.

But from this day forward, I was going to overdose her with love, whether she was able to give it back to me in return or not.

That was the least that I could do.

***

After Sonni's big news, for some reason, I wanted to get out of my parent's house more than ever.

It no longer felt like home.

The house only seemed to remind me of death.

Being that Silas had some friends in real estate, after looking for only two weeks, we found our dream home.

It was my three days off from the hotel, so we were making the big move.

Sure, maybe we should have waited for the actual marriage, but it was soon to come.

I just needed a new home.

A new and fresh start.

And Silas agreed.

Our new home was gorgeous and we would definitely need to have more kids to fill up some of the space.

It wasn't like Carmen's; but still it was an amazing home.

Horizon seemed to love it and I could see Silas and I living there for many years to come.

I even imagined us, sitting on the front porch, smelling like *Bengay*, peeling potatoes and watching out grandchildren playing in the yard.

That vision was everything to me.

"I love you," Silas said with a smile.

Instead of responding, I kissed him.

No, now, he definitely wasn't a perfect man, but I knew without a shout of doubt that he loved me.

I'd seen his temper a time or two and I was sure that if ever pushed to that point, he might come down with the *whoop a bitch's ass* syndrome, but he vowed never to put his hands on me and I believed him; a good seventy-five percent.

Like I said, I could see it in there, somewhere.

But honestly, I would never give him a reason too; which is why I needed to hurry up and get away from the hotel.

If he found out the truth about what I did there, I was sure that it was going to take grace, and maybe a little bit of mace to get his big ass off of me.

So, I was working day and night to find out anything that I could.

I'd been prying about Silas and Carmen's past.

He'd said that when he met her she was already working at the hotel and he said that he'd given her a good bit of money in their divorce, so he wasn't sure why she still worked there.

I guess some of her money probably came from him but I was sure that whatever it was that he'd given her was nowhere near what she'd made from the hotel.

But he made it clear that she didn't have anything when he met her so her riches had to have come after the divorce; whether his money was included in that or not.

He'd said that she had been an average girl and didn't seem to be all about money which was part of the reason why he'd initially pursued her.

So, timeline wise, she must have gotten into the dirty hotel business around what, ten or eleven years ago.

Maybe she had used some of the divorce money to go into business with the "they" that she'd mentioned.

Anything was possible and I was taking every detail that I could back to Detective Wiley.

I was going to get them what they needed even if it killed me.

I continued to go through the boxes as Silas and Horizon headed out to pick up our food.

There was so much to do and so little time to do it.

I headed to the kitchen to start unpacking silverware and plates for us to use once they got back.

I noticed that a box named Silas was on the counter so I carried it to our bedroom.

Now, initially, I wasn't going to be nosey, I really wasn't.

But if curiosity really killed the cat…then consider this cat dead!

I looked into the box.

Just to find that it was a whole bunch of nothing; lots of papers and miscellaneous things, but nothing useful.

I wasn't looking for anything particularly, but something in me was just a tad bit curious about a few things concerning Silas.

But the box seemed to be a dead end.

It was nothing there so it seemed.

Receipts and miscellaneous papers; basically stuff that he should have thrown away a long time ago.

Just as I started to close the box, a vanilla colored paper caught my eye.

I picked it up from under the papers and stared at it.

It was the obituary of Silas's wife and daughter from their double funeral.

Aww, he'd had their funerals together, at the same time.

It was a sweet gesture; but in a weird, sorrowful way.

I had to stare at the photo because the woman was almost identical to Carmen.

I mean, yes they were sisters and all, but they could have passed for twins.

That had to be confusing.

The little girl had been a mixture of the both Silas and her mother.

But how weird was this:

They'd actually named her after *Carmen*.

Why on earth would they do that?

Why on earth would you steal your sister's husband, and then name your child after her?

Talk about a slap in the face!

And I thought my family was all twisted and confused.

Then again, maybe the sister missed Carmen so much that she'd named her daughter after her as a way of trying to regain Carmen's love.

An apologetic gesture?

Maybe.

But obviously, her gesture hadn't worked.

I stared at it a little while longer and just as I was about to put it back into the box, there it was, staring me right in my face.

I looked at it.

I was confused.

What was I really looking at?

The sound of the beeping noise, alerting me that the front door had been opened, forced me to place the obituary back into the box and to sit the box in the corner with the rest of his things.

But I hadn't forgotten what I'd saw.

The date on the obituary said that Silas's wife and daughter had died…only a month before he met me, but he'd told me that they had been dead for over a year.

Why had he lied about something like that?

***

"Did you ever get to see your niece?" I asked Carmen bluntly.

She looked at me as though I had no right to ask her that question.

I couldn't believe that I was only two weeks away from my contract being up.

I'd waited a whole year, and *some change*, and I was so ready.

But in order for things to go as planned, I had to find out anything, everything that I could.

According to the detective, I wouldn't be able to leave until the job was done, so I was all over Carmen like she was my main squeeze.

"I only saw her twice," Carmen said.

"Did you know that her name was Carmen too?" I asked her.

She looked disturbed.

"Who cares? Envy, leave the dead, rotting and stinking…wherever they hell are."

Who says that?

I couldn't believe that a hate so strong actually existed.

But obviously, what Silas and her sister had done had hurt her to the core, so for now, I wouldn't try to reopen those wounds.

At least not right now.

"Have you seen or heard from Silas?" Carmen asked and immediately I shook my head no.

I'd told Silas that I had been getting a lot of *shade* from Carmen at work about our relationship, so I'd asked him to never try to pop up for a visit and to limit his calls while I was at work.

He didn't like it, but I told him to trust me on it and he promised that he would.

I couldn't risk him making things sour between Carmen and I again.

"You still love him don't you?" I asked her.

I had been dying to hear the answer to this question.

"What you call love, I call hate," Carmen answered.

No, what she called hate, I called obsession; but I kept my thoughts to myself.

I knew the truth.

She could deny it if she wanted to.

"So, will you ever leave the hotel?"

"What's with all the questions Envy?"

"I'm just making conversation."

Carmen looked at me.

"Just like you, I'm under a contract. Only mine isn't as simple as yours," was all she said and she walked away from me.

Hmm…so, then what was it?

Later that evening, I sat looking at Silas.

"What are you looking at?"

I didn't say a word.

I hadn't mentioned the obituary yet, but I was about to.

"Remember we said no more lies, right?"

Silas looked at me nervously.

I could immediately tell that he was uncomfortable.

"When did your wife and daughter die?" I asked him.

He looked guilty.

"A month before I met you."

"Why did you lie?"

"Because I didn't want to scare you off. Who would want to talk to a man who had just buried his wife and child? But I had to say something to you. I just had to. It was something about you."

I shook my head and before I could stop myself, I smacked him.

Sure, I had a few lies and secrets in my back pocket, but at least they weren't constantly being exposed.

"I'm sorry. I haven't lied to you since that day that we vowed that we wouldn't. I'd already told that little white lie so I figured that there wasn't any need revisiting it. Please try to understand," Silas begged but I turned my back to him.

He always seemed to have the perfect answer for everything.

But it was all too perfect if you ask me.

Silas tugged at the bottom of my dress.

I refused to look at him, so in one swift motion he flipped me over onto my back.

"Look at me. I'm sorry," he said.

I rolled my eyes at him.

I felt his hand go underneath my dress and he began to tug at my thong.

He placed his other hand below and ripped the thong at its sides.

"I'm sorry," he said again.

I was trying my best to keep my attitude but Silas, and his fingers, weren't making it easy.

In my opinion it was such a stupid lie.

Who lies about when someone dies?

I guess maybe he didn't think that things would go this far, or maybe he didn't think that I would ever find out, but whether it was one reason or the other, it was just plain ole' stupid.

"I'm sorry," Silas said again just before placing his mouth on me.

He knew that I was infatuated with his tongue and that by licking my secret spot was the way to my heart.

I closed my eyes and swarmed as if I wanted him to stop but he knew that I didn't.

It wasn't long after the first few licks that I was begging him to give me just a little bit of pound action.

He entered me quickly and from that moment on, everything else was pretty much a blur.

As I prepared to release my creams of delight, I made up my mind to go ahead and forgive him.

But this was the last time.

For real.

***

Everything was going lovely.

Well, almost everything.

My contract at the hotel ended two days ago…and I was still there.

I'd had to tell Carmen that I wanted to stay a little while longer and boy was I pissed!

And I mean I was as hot as hen's piss pissed!

I was supposed to be gone, free, but because of this stupid case, and because I hadn't gotten much of anything out of Carmen, I was stuck.

And it sucked!

I told Carmen a lie about starting my own boutique and I told her that I wanted to make just a little bit more money.

Of course she knew that just from my *hotel cut*, not including tips, that I'd made quite a bit of money, but she didn't question me.

She'd ripped the contract up in front of me and told me that I was free to leave anytime; with at least a day or two heads-up so that she could take me off of the *menu*.

But I was hoping that I wouldn't have to stay too much longer.

The up side to it all was that Carmen most definitely trusted me, I think, so I was sure that I was going to have what the detective needed soon.

On another note, Silas and I were doing pretty well.

I hadn't asked anymore details after he admitted to lying about when his wife and daughter died.

The only other question I'd asked him was why they'd named their daughter after Carmen.

His response was that it was his wife's idea and that no matter how hard he'd tried to change her mind about it, she wouldn't budge.

Maybe she really had felt bad for what she'd done to her sister.

I wasn't sure.

But all of that was the past, so I tried to stay focused on our future.

And my future with Silas looked brighter than ever.

He was forgiven, and for his sake, he had better hoped that nothing else came up.

We were making plans to go through with him adopting Horizon and changing her last name, and I was definitely excited about that.

Everything was in the works, so basically we would just be waiting on the day that we said "I do."

We were all settled into our new house and our wedding plans were coming along just fine.

I'd tried to move up the date on behalf of Sonni, but she wouldn't let me.

She'd said that she wouldn't want to be in the wedding anyway in her condition and hopefully she would still be alive to see it.

It was weird.

Now that we all knew about the cancer, she was starting to look sicker than ever.

Before she'd told the secret you would have never even guessed it.

I guess she no longer put forth the effort to try and hide it.

We were all trying to support her and be there for her as much as possible.

We'd all watched our Mama go through it, so we knew what to expect, but it still didn't make the process any easier.

We just did the best that we could to make sure that she knew that we all loved her; especially Josephine.

I was sure that it was mostly out of guilt, but Josephine was so far up Sonni's ass that if Sonni passed gas, it came out as Josephine's burp.

She was at her house all the time and she went to Sonni's chemotherapy treatments every chance that she could.

And from what she'd told me, she was going to work out her marriage and that she was no longer going to see Sonni's husband.

And you know what, I believed her.

And I was proud of her.

She was doing the right thing.

Josephine said that she was going to dedicate herself to working on her family and her marriage.

After all, Grant deserved a real chance and she vowed that she would give it to him.

Before I could continue to entertain thoughts about my family, there was a knock on *my room* door.

Ugh, here we go…again.

I was seeing someone new.

He'd reserved me for my whole shift, so I was sure that he was one of those that needed to drink first until he was comfortable or until he was too drunk to stop the process.

"Hi," he said entering.

He looked me up and down.

His eyes damn near fell out of their sockets as he eyed my curves and my hips.

"Damn," he said.

"Yeah, that's what they usually say," I said and walked in front of him, towards the bed, so that he could get a better view from behind.

I looked back to see if he was following me, but he was undressing.

Damn, so maybe he wasn't going to be as nervous as I thought he would be.

I almost smiled at the sight of his package.

It was huge…just the way that I liked it.

"Look, I just served five years in prison. So, in other words, I'm about to fuck the dog shit out of you. Is that okay?"

I laughed aloud but it was on accident.

"Prison?"

We usually only dealt with rich men, so I had to ask.

"Yeah, I took the rap for my boss in a scandal. I got lucky since I didn't have any prior trouble. I only got five years and in return he gave me five million dollars. But he set this whole thing up. He said that he could at least get me a day full of the one thing that I've been missing. So, again, is it okay if I damage that pus---,"

"Yes," I answered without letting him finish his sentence.

I hadn't had anything rough in a while, so I was all in.

I was ready to see what his *pipe* was like and I hoped that he knew how to use it.

He did…

Walking out of the hotel, I turned around quickly.

I had the feeling as though someone was following or watching me.

I mean, I was sure that the detective or one of his employees, were watching from a distance.

But this was different.

I got into my car in a hurry and locked my doors.

As soon as I was settled, my phone started to ring.

It was a number that I didn't recognize.

"Hello?"

At the sound of my voice, the caller hung up.

I called the number back but pulled the phone away from my ear as the white woman spoke.

"The number that you have dialed is no longer in service."

What?

How was that possible when they'd just called me literally seconds ago?

Something just ain't right…

***

I sat in my car, watching my next door neighbors have sex through their window.

Our new home was in a private, quiet community.

I loved it.

It was about an hour away from the hotel, so it was usually late in the evening when I got home.

Silas was pressuring me to quit more than ever but I knew that I couldn't walk away just yet.

But it wouldn't be long.

Carmen was talking to me with no filter and sharing things that I really didn't want to know.

She was allowing me to know things about her personal life and even things that I would consider a little too intimate to share.

Yes, she trusted me, and I was her new best friend.

At least in her mind I was.

Naturally, pretending to like her was actually causing me to find out things about her that I actually did admire.

She had some big future plans and a lot of things that she wanted to do that surprised me.

But not once did I lose focus.

Carmen was going to jail.

It was either her or the both of us.

It was the only way.

I turned my attention back to the neighbors.

The big bay window wasn't covered by blinds or curtains, yet they were going at it as if no one could see them or maybe it was as if they didn't care if anyone saw them at all.

They had just moved in as well, and from chatting with them briefly they seemed like decent people.

But one thing was for sure…they were freaky!

Hopefully not too freaky.

I definitely couldn't handle a repeat of what my deceased past neighbors had put me through.

I forced myself to stop watching them and finally exited the car, only to hear a horn beep behind me.

Quickly I turned around.

Carmen?

What the hell!

I walked to her car in a hurry, quickly glancing back to make sure that Silas had parked in the garage.

Thank goodness, he had.

"Carmen, what are you doing here?" I asked her.

"I followed you. I called you ten times but you didn't pick up," she said.

I rolled my eyes.

I'd wanted to enjoy my ride home in silence so after informing Silas that I was on my way, I placed my phone on silent.

"Why didn't you just beep the horn at me?" I questioned her but she simply shrugged.

Nosey ass.

"Anyway, here you go. I guess you had been messing in your purse or something before you left, and this fell out," Carmen said handing me my license.

I grabbed them from her, still frustrated at the fact that she would follow me for over an hour, all the way home.

If she'd gotten out of the hotel in time to trail me, she surely could have stopped me from leaving and given me my license there.

I surely didn't want her to know where I lived and I surely couldn't risk her finding out that I was still with Silas.

Oh hell, what if he came outside?

"I see you have come a long way from where you used to be. This is a nice house. Hell, you've definitely made enough money at the hotel to be able to afford it. You should thank me. You wouldn't have any of this if it wasn't for me," Carmen said.

Just when you almost try to like her stuck up, inconsiderate, conniving ass, she always reminds you of why you hated her in the first place.

I didn't bother to *thank her* as she'd suggested.

"I have to go," I said to her.

"Go where, you just got home," she said.

"Yeah, I know, but my sister sent a text just as I'd pulled up telling me that I had to come and pick up Horizon tonight," I lied.

"Then why didn't you return my calls if you'd seen them on your phone?"

"I was. Once I was settled. But I have to go. It's already pretty late. Good thing I'm off from the hotel tomorrow," I said and turned my back to her.

"Yeah, good thing. Oh by the way…you should tell your neighbors that they should consider closing the blinds or something; although I did enjoy the little show," Carmen said, just before waving and pulling off.

That woman made my skin crawl.

I got back into my car and headed down the road not far behind her.

Carmen was sneaky, so I wouldn't have been surprised if she would circle back around just to see if I had really gone somewhere or not, so I took a left as she took a right and drove in circles for all of thirty minutes.

Just in case.

I couldn't afford to mess up anything when I was so close to getting what I needed from her.

After I was sure that Carmen was long gone, I finally pulled back into my drive way.

I pressed the button on my keys to open my garage.

I hated to park inside, since usually I was always in a rush, and just parking in the driveway worked better for me, but for tonight, and maybe even from now on, my Toyota was going to be in the garage, and I would make sure that Silas car was always in there too.

Carmen would be back.

Uninvited…and I was sure of it.

***

"Not tonight Silas," I said to him for the third time.

Silas pouted but I was so worn out from the hotel that there was just no way that I could perform my *duties*.

The last week at the hotel had been hell.

I'm assuming that there had been a sudden recruitment of new billionaires or something because I'd had so many new clients, that had paid top dollar to get a taste of Envy's curves.

I'd made over $20,000 in just a week; and that didn't include my tips.

So, now that I was off, I just didn't have anything left to give to Silas.

"But it's been about a week," Silas complained.

"I know. Tomorrow I promise. I'm just so tired."

"I bet you didn't tell them that at the hotel," Silas mumbled.

What?

My eyes opened wide at his statement.

"Who is *them*?" I asked him.

What did he mean by his comment?

Did Silas know the truth about what I was doing at the hotel?

"I was saying them; as in the hotel as a whole. I told you to quit a long time ago. You're basically working for nothing. I don't understand why you're still there Envy. You don't need the money. So what is it? And the hotel is coming in between our relationship. Don't you see that?"

Okay, so we were back on track.

As long as he didn't know that I was a whore, I could take everything else.

I forced myself to sit up.

Silas sat quietly on the edge of the bed.

I was exhausted but I had to get Silas off of my back.

And if sex was the only way to do it, then so be it.

I guess I could understand his frustrations.

The sad part about it all was that he couldn't understand mine.

But pulling him backwards, he laid on his back and I straddled him and forced myself to give him the best ten minutes of his life.

That was all that I had in me, and judging by the smile on his face once he'd released himself inside of me, I was sure that was all that he'd needed.

The next day I didn't wake up until it was almost noon.

And I woke up to an empty house.

I reached for my phone to call Silas to see where he and Horizon had gone off to, but I decided that I was going to enjoy the time alone.

I trusted him with my life and my daughter's life, so I was sure that wherever they were, they were okay.

Carmen had called a time or two and so had the detective.

There were also a few private phone calls but I had been getting those a lot lately.

Along with random numbers that always said that they were disconnected when I called back.

I could be wrong, but something told me that Carmen was behind the mysterious calls.

I just never knew what to expect from her.

I returned the detective's call and he informed me that some of the information that I had given him was leading us in the right direction.

Here recently, Carmen had slipped up and said plenty of things for me to run back and tell him.

Carmen definitely had a problem with alcohol and I got her drunk every chance that I could.

Of course I knew that at the top there was more than one person, but from the way that Carmen talked, if I had to guess, it was either two or three of them at the most.

I was sure that one of them probably had more power, but she talked about them as though they were equal.

She'd also said that the *top dogs* in charge trusted her more than they actually trusted each other.

I definitely found that surprising since Carmen was so unstable.

But maybe they hadn't seen that side of her.

Carmen explained that each the bosses, or head honchos had been there since before she'd become a part of the *team*, and that she didn't know who was in charge of the thirteenth floor before them.

The way that she talked about the people in charge wasn't as though she thought that what they were doing was a bad thing. She talked as though she admired them.

Carmen also expressed that each of them brought very different things to the business and that they were very powerful and rich.

But after saying all of that, and no matter how tipsy she was, she never said their names.

She'd said the names of a celebrity or two, and even a sponsor, but never did she say the name of the bosses in charge of the whole operation.

Carmen described herself as the glue that kept it all together.

She still didn't tell me how she'd exactly gotten into the business but I was working on it.

I was going to get it out of her.

Someone along the way had to have recruited her I suppose.

Maybe the person who hired her at the hotel, or the person that was in her position before her.

I was dying to know how she ended up being the *glue*.

But I was sure that in due time, she would tell me.

Carmen also told me that she was tired of it.

She'd mentioned that she hadn't been on vacation in years and that she just wanted to take her money and run away.

I asked her if she was still under *contract*, like a real one, but all she said was that there was no way that they were going to let her go.

I felt sorry for her, kind of, but oh well, if it were me, she wouldn't give a damn about me.

And I was sure of that.

Not wanting to be bothered, I didn't bother to call Carmen back.

Instead, I headed to the bathroom to run myself a bath.

I was in desperate need of relaxation and I'd be damn if I wasn't going to get it.

Well, at least that was what I'd thought.

My phone started to ring as soon as I was settled in the bathtub.

I scowled myself because I'd forgotten to leave it in my bedroom.

Glancing at it on the rug by the tub, I saw that it was a private number.

Rolling my eyes, I slid down further into the water.

But immediately after the ringing stopped, it started again.

And then again.

And then again.

The private number called back to back until finally I decided to answer it.

"Hello?"

Nothing.

No breathing. No cursing. No comments. No questions.

Just nothing.

They'd called over and over just to say nothing!

Needless to say, I called whoever the speechless person was every kind of bitch, bastard, and everything else I could think of, just before I hung up the phone and turned it completely off.

Idiot!

I was sure that it was Carmen's stupid ass, it just had to be, but I wasn't going to let her ruin my day.

An hour or so later, I got out of the tub and once I was dressed, I turned back on my phone.

As soon as it was up and running, it began to vibrate in my hand.

Another private call.

Frustrated I answered it, but still no one said anything on the other end.

I hung up and sat the phone beside me on the bed.

If it wasn't one thing, it was another, I thought as the private number started to call again.

****

Chapter SIX

I glared at Nolan and his husband with hatred in my heart, as they entered a store.

I was surprised to see them together.

I'd thought that he'd said that he was leaving him but I guess either he was lying, or he was a sucker for love just like everybody else.

I hadn't seen Nolan since that day at the gravesite and I wanted to take my car and run both of them over…and that's exactly what I did.

Okay, so not really.

I only ran them over in my head.

But believe me I really wanted to do it.

Nolan deserved to die for taking the baby from me and his *man* deserved it for telling him to.

But nevertheless, the light turned green, and I drove off, hoping to never see them again.

I stabilized my breathing and headed for the hotel.

I was disappointed to find that all of the parking spaces were filled, where I usually parked, due to a conference being hosted at the hotel, so I had to go find a space under the parking deck in the back.

I got out of the car and before I could even take a step, a big black SUV pulled up and parked directly behind my car.

Something told me to run or at least get back into my car and lock the doors, but like a dummy, I just stood there.

Once I saw who it was, I let out a deep breath.

"Mr. Ben, what are you doing?" I asked him as he stepped in front of his car and then started to approach me.

"Get in the car Envy," he said softly.

I looked at him confused.

"What are you talking about silly," I tried to laugh it off but for some reason I knew that he was serious.

"I've been calling you," he said.

Calling me?

What was he talking about?

He didn't have my number.

Wait a minute…

"You've been the one calling me private and from random numbers?"

He nodded.

"Why?"

He ignored my question.

"That's a nice little house you have too; but I can give you a better one. If you just let me," Mr. Ben said.

What?

He's been to my house?

Old stalking ass!

"Mr. Ben, that's called stalking," I said backing away from him as he continued to come closer and closer to me.

"I love you Envy. Don't you love me?"

"Mr. Ben, you have a wife. I have a family. What we do in the hotel isn't love. What you think you feel for me isn't love," I tried to explain to him.

I could tell by the look on his face that things were about to get ugly.

"Well since you don't love me, it's fairly simple. If I can't have you, no one can. Get in the car Envy," he said and grabbed my arm.

Immediately I started to swing at him.

All I could think to myself was that this could not be happening.

Mr. Ben tightened his grip and I started to scream and looked around for help.

He quickly covered my mouth, wrestled me to the ground and he started to drag me toward his SUV.

I cried, I kicked, I swarmed but no matter what I did, he didn't let up.

He opened the back door and attempted to put me inside.

"Uh uh, I wouldn't do that if I were you."

Mr. Ben paused and I looked towards the voice.

Carmen.

She was pointing a gun at Mr. Ben and from the way that she held it and the comfortable look on her face, I was sure that it wasn't her first time.

I had never been so happy to see someone that I hated in my entire life.

Mr. Ben stared at her and she stared back at him.

But he still didn't free me from his grasp or uncover my mouth.

"Now, we both know that I could shot you, dead, right here and right now, and get away with it. So, it looks like your best bet is to let her go. And then again, it would be nice to let off a little frustration," she said and she pressed something that made a clicking noise.

After another few seconds, which felt like hours, Mr. Ben released me and I ran towards Carmen and stood behind her.

"Now get your ass out of here and don't you ever come back or you will be sorry. Oh, and if I were you, I would watch your back. You know, just in case," Carmen said and without a word, Mr. Ben looked at me one last time, got into his black *Denali*, and sped off.

I was crying uncontrollably.

And before I could stop myself, I hugged Carmen.

But she just stood there.

She didn't say a word or even hug me back.

She just stood there.

Finally she spoke.

"Envy, I am holding a gun you know," Carmen finally said.

I moved in a hurry.

I didn't know what to say.

If it hadn't been for her, there was no telling what would have happened to me.

Maybe he would have killed me or maybe he would just have taken me somewhere far away, away from Silas and away from my little girl.

Never would I have thought that that Mr. Ben was capable of something so extreme.

He'd been stalking me *and* tried to kidnap me.

I was just at a loss of words.

But I had to find a few words to say to Carmen.

In a way, I owed her my life.

"Thank you Carmen. If you hadn't been here…"

"Envy, really, just let it go. Really, it's no big deal," she said and walked to her car that was parked only three spots away, put the gun inside the trunk, and then she came back over to me.

"So you saw the whole thing?"

"Yep. Someone took my parking space, so I was just sitting there, waiting to go in. And then I saw his stupid ass," she said.

I wondered what had taken her so long to come to my rescue but I guess that really didn't matter.

As long as she'd come.

We walked towards the hotel and she started talking business as though nothing had happened.

What's wrong with this woman?

I allowed her to talk but my mind was still on what had just happened to me.

She coached me to wipe the tears from my eyes and to fix my face before entering the hotel.

I walked through the doors, and immediately turned around and walked back out.

I sat on the sidewalk, right and front of the hotel.

I thought that Carmen was going to come to see about me, but of course she didn't.

But I didn't care.

That was the last straw.

I had to get away from this place…now!

***

"Look," Carmen said and nodded towards the television in her office.

It was Mr. Ben being led in handcuffs to a police car.

The headline said: "Billionaire accused of wife's murder."

He'd killed his wife?

Because of me?

The television said that she'd been dead for weeks.

I just didn't know what to say, so without saying anything, and since it was the end of my shift, I got the hell out of the hotel as fast as possible.

I hadn't wanted to be there in the first place.

Once inside my car, I tried to get my thoughts together.

In a strange way, I felt partly responsible for the death of his wife.

He had done it because of me; because he was in love with the things that I did to him.

And now an innocent woman; a wife and a mother was dead.

All because of me.

I felt as though I was about to have some kind of breakdown, so I drove home as fast as I could.

Carmen called me over and over and even Detective Wiley called me a time or two, but I just wanted to get home.

I just needed to be home.

I'd told Detective Wiley about the incident, but he'd sworn that his men hadn't seen anything.

I arrived home and I couldn't wait to get inside.

It was early in the afternoon, so of course Silas wasn't there, but that was okay.

I locked the front door and ran to my bedroom and then headed for the closet.

I got as far behind a few bags and still unpacked boxes that I could go and I just sat there.

I just sat there and cried.

I cried like never before.

So many things were wrong and I just wanted everything to be right.

I needed the advice of Mama and one of her soothing hugs too.

She would know just what to say.

She would know just what to do.

And then it hit me.

Maybe there was a way to reach her and I did something that I hadn't done in forever.

I started to pray.

***

"What?"

I needed him to speak slower so that I could understand what he was saying.

"She's gone. It happened two nights ago. She'd made me promise not to say anything until I had her cremated. It was her dying wish. I promised her that I would do it. I didn't want to but I promised," Sonni's husband, Mark, cried.

I sat down on the edge of the bed.

Immediately, Silas noticed that something was wrong and came to my side.

Sonni was gone.

I had already been feeling so down lately, and this was just going to make everything worse.

"She left letters, explaining it all and requesting that you guys don't take it out on me and that I was only doing what she asked. I tried to talk her out of it, especially with the baby situation and how Nolan didn't bother to tell you, but she said she didn't want anyone crying over her lifeless body. She'd said that she didn't deserve it. And she didn't want a funeral or memorial service. She requested that we each have a small urn of her ashes. I have them here."

I wanted to cry, but I couldn't.

I just felt…empty.

But the fact that she wasn't hurting and suffering anymore made my heart smile through the pain.

I hated that she hadn't let any of us be there with her, but she'd had her husband by her side just like she'd wanted.

I listened to him speak for a few seconds more and he'd said that he was calling to break the news to Josephine next.

I already knew that her guilty heart was probably going to take it pretty hard so I told him that I would do it instead.

"What's wrong? Sonni?" Silas asked.

"Yes. She's gone," I said softly as Silas embraced me.

For some strange reason I wondered if he thought that people died too much in this family.

Hell I was starting to feel the same way.

But hopefully there would be no more deaths, no time soon.

I was going to add that little request into my new daily and nightly prayer routine.

I'd wanted to tell him what had happened to me at the hotel, but I knew for sure that he wouldn't have allowed me to go back.

He would have made me quit and then I would have been going to jail with everyone else.

But I wanted to tell him so badly, so that he could comfort me, and I wished that I had somebody that I could be one hundred percent honest with, so that I could get some of the things that I was feeling off of my chest.

Talking to Carmen about it was like talking to a damn door, so I was going to have to figure it all out on my own.

Mark vowed to drop off my personal urn of Sonni's ashes later on that evening and strangely I couldn't wait to get them in my hands.

As I hugged Silas, I had a small vision of Sonni, Tia and the baby in Heaven.

I didn't see my parents, but I knew that they were there somewhere.

But my sisters and nephew were smiling and laughing and it was as if they were all looking at me with eyes that told me that I shouldn't feel sad for them.

They were just fine.

I was the one still stuck here on Earth while they were in paradise.

With that thought in mind, I kissed Silas and told him that I couldn't wait to get married and have another baby.

Life was just too short.

And there just wasn't any more time to waste.

The wedding and baby were the next things on my list.

Maybe or maybe not in that order.

***

"Why are you wearing that ring?" Carmen pointed out.

Damn it!

I forgot to take it off.

Hiding Silas from Carmen was a lot harder than I thought that it would be.

And I was sure that it was because I loved him so much.

With almost being kidnapped and the death of Sonni, I had been leaning on Silas more than ever and he had been right there.

He never left my side.

If I was up crying at three o'clock in the morning, he was up too, right beside me, telling me that everything was going to be okay.

If I was mad at the world and walking around the house screaming, and cussing because at times I just felt so lost, Silas was right there, following behind me, picking up everything that I threw along the way.

And my love for him was growing stronger than ever and I was so consumed by it that I wanted the whole world to know about it.

Well, except for Carmen.

I had so many mixed feelings about her, which always had me confused and stressed out.

I mean, the woman had saved my life; that just had to count for something.

But still yet, if I didn't do my part in bringing her and the hotel down, I would go down with them.

But again…this woman saved my freaking life!

So, it wasn't fun to be in my shoes.

Detective Wiley said that all of the information that I'd given him was turning out to be accurate and they were so close to cracking the case, they just needed a little bit more.

Something a little bit stronger.

And it was up to me to get it.

I knew that once it was all said and done that I would be free, married, pregnant and probably happier than ever.

I mean, I just didn't have a choice but to do what I had to do.

But how do you ruin the life of someone that saved yours?

It just didn't seem right.

But, I had to stay on it if I wanted my freedom.

And I couldn't make such a big mistake like wearing my ring in front of Carmen again.

"Um, I put it on this morning. It's so pretty and to be honest, though I can't be with him, I miss him," I said to Carmen.

Maybe she would give me a little sympathy.

"Well, that's because you haven't tried to date anyone else Envy. I mean, sure you get dick on the regular, but it's not the same as love and all of that other stuff. Trust me, I know. But to wear the ring…that's just tacky," she said and walked away.

Immediately I took it off.

I wiped my forehead.

That was a close one.

Though I hated even coming to the hotel, I was there, and I headed towards my room so that I could breath.

It was empty.

I'd told Carmen that from now on, especially since the incident with Mr. Ben that I only wanted to be ordered once a day.

For some reason, I'd thought that things had to go according to how they were when I was on contract but on a drunken night, Carmen called my phone wanting to talk and she actually questioned me as to why I still took so many clients when I didn't have to.

I'd never even thought of it that way.

I was no longer obligated by the contract to be at the hotel.

I was only there to try to keep my ass out of jail and because the detective said that I had to be, so I'd told her the very next day that I would only see one client a day; and that even applied to being reserved.

Carmen hadn't fussed about it either.

I mean after all, what could she say?

She couldn't make me do it, or I would just say that I was done and for the most part I was sure that she just wanted to keep me around.

After all, her drunk ass mentioned on plenty occasions that I was her *only* friend.

But she was wrong…I was actually her enemy.

Even though I was still disgusted to have to still be there, the whole one client thing was making things a lot better for me.

I didn't feel so mentally, emotionally, or sexually drained.

And I was able to keep Silas happy, regularly.

I was always home extra early and I'd told Silas that I'd gone down to part-time at the hotel.

I'd told him some bull crap about just being used to working and doing things all on my own for the last few years that I had to wing myself away from having to work.

But since I was home more and overdosing him with *the pussy*, he rarely complained these days.

Carmen questioned if my decision was the best one, money wise, since she thought that I was only there to keep getting money to open up a business, but I already had a hell of a lot of money.

I knew that one day I was going to have to find a way to explain the money to Silas.

Since I hid it most of the time, and since Silas had enough money for the both of us, I hardly every spent a dime of my own money.

Secretly, I was one wealthy woman and at some point I was going to have to start enjoying the money that I'd had to lay on my back and earn.

It was only right.

Hell, it couldn't just sit there, untouched, forever.

I just had to find the perfect lie to explain the dough to my future husband.

But I would cross that bridge after I was away from the hotel and done getting the detective what he needed.

For some reason, I wondered if Carmen was really in the dark about Silas and I or if she was just playing along.

You just never know what she was thinking or what she had up her sleeve.

But soon enough it wouldn't matter.

My short day at the hotel was over before I knew it and I headed to meet Josephine.

Josephine was definitely different these days; especially since we'd lost Sonni.

She took it pretty hard of course but afterwards, she decided to make a few lifestyle changes.

She was on a diet and losing weight.

She was also planning to renew her wedding vows with Grant.

I was happy that she was actually keeping her word and staying as far away from Sonni's *used to be* husband as she could.

Well, not that she had much of a choice in the matter anyway.

Only a week after Sonni's death, Mark packed up the kids and he moved somewhere towards the west coast.

All he'd said was that he had family out that way and he and the kids were going to try their best to get through life without Sonni.

He promised to keep in touch and vowed to send the kids down for summers and holidays.

And I was sure that he would keep his word.

I kept the urn of Sonni's ashes right beside my bed.

The sudden closeness of our relationship before she'd died made me miss her a lot more than I expected to.

But at least I still had Josephine.

Josephine was meeting me to shop for a dress.

The wedding wasn't all that far away and I still hadn't found a dress.

And with these curves and hips of mine, I knew that whatever dress I chose, it would need weeks of alterations, so I had to get on it.

"Hi gorgeous," Josephine squealed and embraced me.

I smiled at her and hugged her.

She was looking sexier than ever.

She was showing off her curves and she'd changed her hair back to how she used to wear it years ago.

Yes!

She had better work it!

I smacked her booty as we entered the dress shop but suddenly I got this eerie feeling.

I couldn't quite explain it but I felt as though I was being watched, again, so I checked my surroundings.

And just as I suspected…Carmen.

Okay, so this whole stalking thing was out of control!

Maybe she and Mr. Ben were related or something; stalking must have run in their family.

It wasn't okay!

It was crazy!

Besides, she was supposed to still be at the hotel.

Why was she sitting outside the dress shop?

My phone started to ring, but instead of answering it, I headed back out the door.

"Carmen why in the hell are you following me?"

"I'm not following you. I was just passing through and saw your car, so I decided to stop," Carmen lied.

Yeah right!

She was definitely following me…again.

"Carmen, you are acting like a stalker. And it's starting to freak me out and piss me off all at the same time. It's crazy Carmen. Look, yes we're cool and all but stop showing up uninvited," I said to her and turned my back to her.

"What are you doing here Envy?" she asked as though she hadn't cared about anything I'd said.

"If you must know, my sister is renewing her wedding vows and she's looking for a dress. I will call you later, okay," I said, trying to sound nice as I went back inside of the shop.

I didn't care if she'd saved my life or not, she had to go!

I was trying to keep my cool and be nice to her but she really did need some type of help.

She really needed to see someone about her issues.

I was starting to think that prison might not be the best place for her.

She needed to be in a place with folks of her *kind*.

After about thirty minutes and seeing out of the window that Carmen had no intentions of pulling off, instead of me trying on dresses, I had to convince Josephine to try on a few, since Carmen was watching.

I briefly had to explain the situation, or at least what I wanted Josephine to know about it.

I was so frustrated but I knew that I couldn't react the way that I wanted to, which made me so mad that I almost wanted to cry.

I knew that I still had work to do and that I still *needed* Carmen in order to do it.

So, I was just going to have to put up with Carmen and all of her crazy ways.

I just didn't have a choice.

It wasn't until we exited the store that Carmen pulled off.

Absolutely ridiculous!

She was insane and she had no shame at all.

Lord I wasn't going to make it too much longer under these conditions, so it was time to turn things up a notch, or I was going to end up just as crazy as she was; or in the jail cell right next to hers because I couldn't get the job done.

Suddenly, all of the mixed emotions about throwing her under the bus because she'd saved me were gone.

Carmen's ass was going down!

And I still didn't have a damn wedding dress!

***

"Let's get away soon; just the two of us. It'll be sort of a pre-honeymoon type of thing," Silas suggested.

It was late fall and winter was soon to make *her* presence known, so somewhere warm was just what I needed.

I hadn't been on a vacation in years.

About two years or so before Keymar died to be exact.

We'd gone to the beach and it was a week that I was sure that I would never forget.

We walked and talked on the beach all night long.

He'd told me how special I was and how lucky he was to have me.

He'd told me everything that any woman wanted and deserved to hear.

But come to think of it, it had to be around the time that Marie, his other child's mother, had popped up pregnant.

Apparently he hadn't meant a thing that he'd said.

He was just trying to ensure that he had me wrapped around his little finger just in case he was exposed.

Love can be such a tricky thing.

You can think you have it and feel like you have it, but you just never know what the other person involved is really up to.

I'm assuming that's where trust comes in but then that brings about this question:

Can you ever really trust someone?

Maybe.

And then again, maybe not.

"Did you hear me?"

I looked at Silas.

I loved him.

I really did---enough to spend the rest of my life with him.

Did I trust him?

Not one hundred percent.

It was obvious that he had a couple of secrets but so did I.

We were just two imperfect people trying to find a perfect love.

And I was okay with that.

"Yes baby, somewhere warm would be nice. I haven't been on a beach in forever," I said with a smile and kissed him.

Maybe we could make a couple of new memories and hopefully they would last forever.

He told me that he would plan everything and then squeezed my *tits*, and walked away.

I couldn't do a thing but laugh.

Boy, did I love that man!

I headed to shower.

I was going out to dinner with Carmen for the second time this week.

She was all over me…like always.

She called all the time and when I wasn't with a client at the hotel, I couldn't get her to shut up.

She still never apologized for her stalker issues, and I was sure that she didn't plan to.

At this point, it was pointless to even worry about it…I just had to learn how to get around it.

But tonight I was hoping that she would give me something good; good enough for the police to use.

I was ready to get it all over and done with so that I could peacefully go on with my life.

And I was close.

I could feel it.

Being around Carmen, I'd learned a few things about style and I'd updated my wardrobe.

Though I had plenty of money to do so, I'd let Silas take me shopping.

Of course he'd allowed me to buy anything that I wanted, with no questions asked, worries or complaints.

Don't get me wrong, money and all, I was still cheap.

I checked every price tag, on everything, and if it was way too high, it stayed where it was.

I learned from Carmen that the key to any outfit was to accessorize.

A twenty dollar dress with the right accessories, shoes and bag, could go a long way.

So, tonight I was wearing an all-black top and skirt outfit that I'd found on clearance, with a single two-carat gold and diamond bangle, one hell of a gold diamond necklace, and black Dolce and Gabbana stilettos with a matching clutch, which I'd actually gotten from the hotel.

I looked like a pocket full of money, but I had to in order to step out with Carmen.

I knew that no matter what I threw together, she was probably going to still look ten times better but I wasn't too far behind her.

Though she knew where I lived, I still didn't allow her to come to my home, so I headed to the restaurant in a hurry.

When I arrived, Carmen waved for me to head over to the table.

She stood up to show off her all white pants jumpsuit that was accessorized with everything gold.

Even her shoes were gold.

I had to give it to her…the bitch was *fly*!

Just like always.

"Hey," she said.

I smiled at her.

I was getting used to having what most called a *girl-friend*, outside of my sisters.

I was even a lot more casual with the women on the thirteenth floor, but our conversations never went outside of work.

Hell, even then, they could barely talk to me because Carmen was always in my damn face.

So, the outings with Carmen were actually very different for me and I kind of liked it.

I knew that once she was gone that I was going to have to make a friend or two.

Though Silas didn't have family in town, he had a host of friends.

I'd had the pleasure of meeting a few of them.

They all seemed happy and most of them were married.

I promised that we could double date with some of them soon and as soon as Carmen was out of my hair, I was going to fulfill some of those promises.

Some of the wives seemed pretty cool and were maybe even *friend material*.

But as for tonight, it was all about Carmen.

"You look good enough to eat," Carmen complimented me.

I was sure that she had a *thing* for women but I dared not ask her.

"Thank you. And you look great as always," I said taking my seat.

We chatted briefly and then ordered our food but before we could spark up another conversation, Carmen's phone started to ring.

Usually she stepped away, but tonight she didn't.

"Yes?" she asked.

I tried to pretend as though I wasn't listening and started to fiddle with my phone but my ears were straining to hear just even a little of what the other caller was saying.

I could hear that it was a man's voice, but that was about it.

"Yes, more than the usual. Yes. Everything is set. No. I'm not. Yes it will be."

Carmen was very short with her answers as though she was already on to me and pretty much knew that I was trying to listen.

It was obvious that it was a business call, hotel business I was sure, but her words were short and simple.

"Okay. And I have to talk to you about a replacement. Bye," Carmen hung up.

A replacement?

Was she trying to get out?

But she was too late.

The police were already on to her and if no one else was going down, she was.

And I had to make sure of that in order to ensure my own freedom.

"Everything okay?" I asked.

She didn't respond, only waited for the waiter to place the Scotch in front of her.

She was pissed off, I could tell.

"I hate men."

I looked at her.

"Men think they can do it all on their own when really they are nothing without a woman. Whether it's on a personal or professional level, they need us. It's time that they admit it. Damn!" Carmen said and swallowed her drink in less than two seconds.

"The men in my life suck. They have always sucked," she said and looked as though she was about to cry.

She wasn't drunk yet, but I was sure that she was about to go *deep* on me and I was all ears.

"It seems like every man in my life or that I come across reminds me of him. He's the reason that I hate men. Because I hated him."

"Who is him?" I asked her, though I already knew that she was talking about Silas.

"My father."

Oops---I was wrong.

I remembered that Carmen had said that her mother had killed her dad when she was younger but somehow she'd gotten off on the charges and away with it.

Carmen always seemed uncomfortable when she talked about it and I knew that she took his death pretty hard.

"How was your father? What was he like?"

"He was like the Devil…from the hood. If I had to describe him in one word, the word would be evil. He was awful to my mother. Awful to my siblings and awful to me. He'd deserved to die; which is why I killed him."

What?

Wait a minute.

Time out!

I thought she'd told me that her mother killed her father.

But now she was saying that she killed him…huh?

But honestly, I couldn't say that I was surprised.

As I said, she'd looked extremely comfortable holding that gun when she was pointing it at Mr. Ben, so I was sure that she'd done it before.

"He was beating my mama one night and after listening to her scream for what seemed like forever, something in me snapped. It's like I'd had an outer body experience. I wasn't myself for those few minutes. I was someone else. But I ran to the kitchen, grabbed a knife and I entered their bedroom. And without so much as a second thought, I stabbed him. I only stabbed him once, in the back, but once was all that it had taken. Mama and I both watched him die without even attempting to help him. Of course she wiped my prints off of the knife and she took the blame. Thankfully she'd got off or I would have never forgiven myself. But hell, I found it hard to forgive her for even putting us in that situation and for keeping us in it for so long. All she'd had to do was leave. She would tell others that it just wasn't that easy but at the time, I just didn't understand. Anyway, the sad part was that after that day, I was changed forever. I was never the same. The only thing that stayed the same was my hate for men. Well, it's like I will somewhat love them...but I hate them too. It's hard to explain," Carmen said.

I sat with my mouth open and Carmen reached over and closed it as the waiter came back to the table.

Well, she hadn't shot him like I'd assumed, but stabbing him was just as bad.

I'd always known that some things in her past made her who she was, but I definitely didn't sign up for these types of confessions!

"I'd been dying to get that off of my chest. I trust that you won't tell a soul. Thanks for being my friend Envy," Carmen said, smiled as though she hadn't just confessed to murder and then she started in on her meal.

She put the C in crazy.

I wasn't sure if this was something that I was going to tell the detective or not.

It didn't really pertain to the case, at least not this one, so I figured that I'll keep her little secret, this time.

But I wasn't her friend.

For her sake I wished that I was, but I wasn't.

The rest of the night went by slowly, but it wasn't a miserable time.

As I said, I often found myself enjoying Carmen's company, as long as she was *wasted*, but I was always focused.

Sure my conscious would kick in here and there, and I would feel bad, just a little bit, but if the shoe was on the other foot, there was no doubt in my mind that Carmen would be doing the same thing.

And that thought alone made me feel just a little bit better.

Just a little.

****

Chapter SEVEN

"Look, ride it or get off of it!"

The client screamed at me from below me.

See, this is why I had to get the hell away from this place!

It was so frustrating that I was still there taking the disrespect and being treated like some floozy when I didn't have to be.

Detective Wiley was constantly breathing down my neck for more information that I still didn't have.

So I was still in the same situation.

Fewer dicks on a daily basis---but the same amount of humiliation and disrespect.

Well, not all of the clients were assholes; only the new ones, or the ones that I'd seen a time or two.

But a few bad apples always spoil the bunch.

"All these curves and ass but you scared to take some dick?" he asked and pushed me off of him and forced me onto my back.

I didn't know what the hell he was talking about but I was the best.

I never got complaints and I knew without a shout of a doubt that I did everything top notch.

There were plenty of men that would agree on that.

Maybe he was just used to something different.

I wasn't sure, but I was ready to get this whole thing done and over with.

This was my last day for a whole week.

Silas and I were going on vacation and I just couldn't wait.

Though I wasn't supposed to, I'd told Carmen that when I got back that I would work only one more week and then I was done.

I just couldn't do the hotel thing anymore.

So when I got back, I was going to do whatever it takes, in a week's time, to find whatever it was that I needed to find and I was getting the hell out of there.

I'd tried to get it from Carmen and I had got some things but not enough.

So, I was going for paperwork.

I didn't even care if she caught me or whatever; I was going to get what I needed.

If I had to beat her ass and drag the whole filing cabinet out of the hotel, I was going to find what I needed and that was that.

Of course Detective Wiley wasn't happy about me taking a week off but I told him that I needed a break and I was going to have one.

I also told him of my plans for when I returned.

I wasn't playing around anymore.

Not with the hotel.

Not with Carmen.

And not with these cheating, disrespectful ass clients either.

The client rammed his penis inside of me as though he was trying to make a point.

I looked at him confusedly, yet my mouth was trained to fake moan whether I was enjoying the moment or not.

To be honest, he was just giving himself a work out.

I could barely feel a thing.

But I could see that he had something to prove so I pretended to let him prove it.

Maybe his woman cheated on him or something and he had to prove to himself that he still had it or whatever.

After he'd pumped himself damn near to death, finally he released himself and jumped off of me as though he'd just committed a crime.

Without saying a word, he got dressed and slammed something down on the table by the door just before walking out of it.

I got myself together, straightened up the room and went to get what I thought was a tip.

It was…one dollar bill.

Bastard!

Oh well, I would get a decent cut from Carmen anyway, but the whole ordeal just confirmed that I would do anything necessary to get out of the *game*.

It was time for me to go.

Point. Blank. Period.

I headed to shower and of course Carmen was waiting for me once I was dressed.

"So are you excited about your family trip?" Carmen asked.

I'd told her that I was going on a family getaway.

Carmen was so damn nosey that I had to make sure that all of the basics were covered.

Josephine was keeping Horizon and they were actually driving up to visit her husband Grant's family in Washington D.C. for a few days.

So just in case Carmen had something up her sleeve, they would be gone too and all would look legit.

I wouldn't be surprised if Carmen had done some kind of background check on me and knew where everyone in my entire family lived.

I was sure that she had because crazy people do crazy things.

I nodded at her as she headed down the elevator with me, still chatting.

I thought that she was going to stop once we got to the downstairs office, but she didn't.

She continued to talk and walked outside with me.

I pretended to be listening to her and I couldn't wait for her sentence to come to an end so that I could tell her I had to go but the sudden screech of tires turned both of our attention to the street.

Two cars almost collided but thankfully the cars stopped just inches from each other.

"Oh my goodness! I almost had a flashback of…"

Carmen cut her sentence short.

I looked at her.

Of what?

"Of what?" I asked her.

She didn't say anything.

She just pretended to be paying attention to the two cars.

"Of what?"

She looked at me.

It was almost as if she was trying to see if I was really a friend or a foe.

I smiled at her and tried to look sincere.

But I was dying to know what she had to say next.

"A flashback of the accident that killed my so-called sister and my niece," Carmen said with disgust.

What?

A flashback of the accident?

So she was there?

"What do you mean?"

I could tell that she didn't want to have the conversation.

"I was there. I'd spotted them coming out of a store and I followed them. I was just curious as to where they were going. I hadn't seen my sister in years and that was only the second time that I'd seen the girl. I was just wondering where they would go next. so I just followed them. But only a minute or two later down the road, the car came out of nowhere and hit them head on. I saw the whole thing. It was like something that you saw on a movie. The way that they'd collided I knew that everyone was dead.

But I didn't stop to help or stop to see. I just drove away. They got what they deserved," Carmen said.

Oh, this woman was sick and twisted in the inside!

There was no way that I could have watched my own flesh and blood, die, and then just drive away as though I hadn't seen a thing.

No matter the hurt, angry, hate or pain, I just couldn't believe that Carmen could do something like that.

But then again, Carmen was something else.

I'd felt my share of hate before, but I was scared of Carmen's level of hate.

I never wanted to feel like that about anybody.

I didn't bother to comment to what she'd said, instead, I said goodbye and told her to call me if she needed me, though I didn't really mean it.

Once inside of my car, I thought about what Carmen had said.

I wondered how Silas would feel if he knew that Carmen had seen the accident and hadn't tried to help.

Who knows…maybe they weren't dead just yet.

Maybe one of them could have lived or needed something as simple as CPR and all Carmen would have had to do was get out of the car and assist.

But she hadn't.

Her heart was as cold as ice and she didn't love anybody; not even herself.

Driving down the road, I figured that it was really nothing to tell Silas. so I would just let it be.

There was no point in opening old wounds, especially since we were about to be on vacation.

With the beaches of the Bahamas on my mind, I shook away all of the negative and agonizing thoughts and allowed myself to focus on positivity and my pre-honeymoon.

It was time for some fun in the sun and boy was it long overdue!

***

It was day two in the Bahamas and I was having so much fun, that it all felt like a dream.

It was a dream come true and I never wanted to wake up from it.

Everything was so perfect!

The island was so beautiful.

The people on it were beautiful.

And the man by my side was beautiful.

I truly felt like the luckiest woman in the world and I was enjoying every minute of it.

"I love you baby," Silas chimed as we sat on the beach, looking up at the moon.

"Oh, I love you too. So much, I really do," I responded to him.

I almost became emotional because I just couldn't believe that I was in this place or in this space in time and in my life.

A few years ago I would have never even thought that I would be somewhere enjoying something like this.

I could barely pay my bills and now I was in the Bahamas.

And I had a man by my side that loved me.

He showed it in every way and every day and though some things were questionable, his love wasn't one of them.

The way he loved me was unexplainable.

And I couldn't wait to be his wife.

I looked around the beach to see how many people were there.

It was a few scattered folks here and there, but none were too close to us.

I proceeded to unzip his kakis and he looked at me as though I was crazy but he didn't stop me.

I touched him and at the warmth of my hand, his manhood started to swell.

I stroked it for only a while and soon after, I swallowed it whole.

Hey…we might as well make this a vacation that we would never forget.

***

"I don't want to go back," I whined to Silas.

It was our last day in the Bahamas and we were enjoying lunch before it was time for us to leave.

I'd enjoyed myself so much that I told him that we absolutely had to come back someday.

Maybe not for our real honeymoon, but someday in the near future.

I felt so at peace while there and it was as if I didn't have a care in the world.

Nothing was on my mind the entire time but peace, love, joy and happiness and I just wished that things could always be that way.

But reality was calling…and so was Carmen.

She'd called a couple of times but I hadn't answered.

Whether she wanted to discuss something personal or business, once I got off that plane and encountered such beauty, I decided that I didn't want to be bothered with anything or anybody back in North Carolina.

Well, except checking up on Horizon of course.

Silas and I finished our lunch and then we headed back to the hotel to prepare to leave.

After making love one last time, with all of our things, we headed to the airport only to find out that our flight had been delayed.

Silas had brought his laptop along and said that he could sit and take care of a few things.

Since we had a few hours, I told him that I was going back out to visit a few places that I hadn't been able to get to.

I promised that I would be back plenty of time before it was time to board the plan, so Silas agreed and I headed on my way.

I really wanted to stay.

The people were friendly and seemed so happy.

It seemed as though they had a natural high; no weed or alcohol needed.

But I liked it.

My curls were blowing wildly in the wind and disobedient hairs tickled my nose.

I giggled as I entered the store.

I started grabbing any and everything that I could carry.

I wanted as many memories of this place as possible.

Finally calling it quits, I carried all of my merchandise to the counter.

The chocolate stallion of a man stared at me the entire time that he scanned my items, so my flirty ass winked.

If I was single, he could have considered *his bones jumped*, but since I wasn't, I would just smile and be a little flirty.

I grabbed my wallet from my purse but just as I went into it to pull out *Silas's* bank card, something caught my attention.

I listened attentively to what was going on and what was being said at the counter beside of me.

Anger started to stir up inside of me and after a while I could no longer keep my cool.

As the cashier waited for my payment, I headed over to the lady beside me instead.

I tapped her on the back and she turned to face me.

"Sonni?" I said to my sister who was supposed to be dead.

She looked at me as if she didn't know me and soon after she spoke.

"I'm sorry but you have me confused with someone else. My name is Savannah," *my sister* said.

****

Chapter EIGHT

"Savannah my ass! What are you doing here Sonni? You're supposed to be dead!" I yelled furiously.

Sonni finished paying for her things and then proceeded to walk out of the store.

I didn't bother to pay for mine and I followed behind her.

Outside she walked as though she didn't know that I was following her.

Itching to whoop her ass, I grabbed her arm and forced her to face me.

"What the hell is going on Sonni?"

She let out a deep breath in frustration.

Finally she walked to a bench and sat down.

"Sonni, what the hell is going on here?" I asked her for the last time.

"I faked my death, what does it look like Envy?"

Bitch!

Who does that?

And furthermore, whose damn ashes was I talking to every damn day?

I had so many questions and she was going to answer them and she was going to answer them right damn now!

"So you didn't or don't have cancer?"

"Hell no. I'm as healthy as an ox. It was just all a part of my plan to disappear. I hated having to shave my head but I figured that eventually it would grow back. Even those fake chemotherapy treatments that Josephine thought that she was accompanying me to were all a scheme. Let's just say a lot of people owed me a few favors. It was the perfect plan," Sonni said.

I looked at her in disbelief.

I just didn't understand.

"Why Sonni? Why?"

"Why not? There are plenty of reasons why. I just wanted out. I just wanted to be free. No husband. No kids. No family. Just me. Living the normal life or the life that everybody else wanted to live, just didn't work for me. I was miserable. When I said that I don't love anyone, like I was or am supposed to; I meant it. But many people hate the truth. But it is *my* truth. I also faked my death to get away from my crazy lover who couldn't accept the fact that I didn't love him either," Sonni said.

What?

It just broke my heart that she hated us all so much that she would have rather we think that she was dead than to actually live life enjoying us.

What happened to her?

Why had she been made this way?

I just didn't understand.

And Sonni was also having an affair too?

I guess that's the real reason that she didn't care that he was sleeping with Josephine.

"Sonni, I just don't understand all of this," I said aloud.

"It's not meant for you to understand. You were never supposed to find out. I had it all worked out. A few friends of mine had everything covered and did everything just right. You and the others were never supposed to know. Only the people involved in the plan, myself, and my husband of course."

What?

Mark, Sonni's ex, current, or whatever husband, knew about this?

"Mark knew about this?"

"Of course he did. The plan wouldn't have worked without him."

"And he agreed to this stupid ass plan?" I said angrily.

"Of course he did. We didn't love each other. I never truly loved him and he'd fallen out of love with me a long time ago. And besides…I paid him. Whether you believe it or not, everybody has a price and anyone can be bought," Sonni said.

I was sick and tired of dealing with crazy people!

She was just as crazy as everybody else.

"Paid him? Paid him for what? His silence? But why? And you guys have, or had, plenty of money with the company so why would he agree to something like this for money?"

Sonni looked at me as if she'd never seen anyone so stupid in her whole entire life.

"Honey that business flopped years ago. We were broke and in debt."

Huh?

"Why didn't you say anything?" I asked her.

"Say something to who---you? How where you going to help me? Besides, I found a way to fix it all on my own."

"How?"

She laughed out loud.

It was the creepiest laugh I'd ever heard.

"By doing the same thing that you do," she said with a straight face.

What the hell did she mean by that?

"Your first day at the hotel, the day that you signed your contract, was my last day at the hotel."

You have got to be kidding me!

"I would mostly stay my four days *on*, at the hotel, on the thirteenth floor, because after all, it is a long drive from there to back home. We were going to move back to Charlotte, but Carmen said that staying at the hotel wasn't a problem. As long as she could sell my ass during work hours, she didn't care. And even some nights, she would need me to fill in if someone couldn't make it in. I would only leave the hotel late in the evenings; when I was sure that you were gone, and home with Horizon by then. I was always on edge about running into you, but I never did. I never even saw you. I'd actually thought you'd quit or something until that day. That day, you followed Carmen and walked right passed me without even looking in my direction. But I knew from those curves and hips, without even seeing your face, at first, that it was you. Anyway, one of their connections had done business with me in the past and when he heard about my financial troubles, he offered to help. And by helping he sent me in Carmen's direction. I'd gone by the name *Savannah*, at the hotel. Savannah has always been a part of me. Savannah *is* me. And I *am* Savannah. I used to deny that *she* existed, and it took me years to accept that Savannah lived inside of me. She was in my mind and in my heart. She's the only *person* that has ever understood me. So, finally, I stopped fighting her and learned to embrace her. Life is so much easier *with* her," Sonni said.

What the hell was she talking about?

And who in the hell was Savannah?

Was Savannah a person, an imaginary friend or what?

Ok so, Sonni was bipolar?

Or was she schizophrenic?

Or did she just have multiple personalities?

I was so confused.

But even more than confused, I was sad.

I'd never known just how sick she was until now and I'd failed her as a big sister.

I knew something was wrong, but I didn't know that it was this.

"As I said I'd done a few favors when business was good to earn a few friends for life, so I had them make me a fake ID and social to match. I just didn't want any ties to that place. So if you've ever mentioned my name, my real one, Carmen wouldn't know that we were related; unless she noticed that we kind of look alike. Anyway, I made plenty of money and enough to pay off every debt that we had. Of course, Mark knew what I was doing and never questioned me as long as I brought home the *bacon*. He

screwed Josephine and I screwed the men at the hotel. I'd
thought that I was doing it for my family. I was trying so
hard to be normal. But I finally realized that I didn't really
care about anyone other than myself. After leaving the
hotel, somehow one of my regulars became obsessed with
me. Mr. Ben. Have you ever screwed him? Honey, he just
wouldn't leave me alone. He threatened to kill me if I
didn't see him or sleep with him. For a while I still had sex
with him, just for the money, but when I couldn't give him
what he wanted, he started acting insane. So, I developed
the cancer lie to throw him off too. And slowly but surely
since he thought that I was dying, he started to back off. I
figured that maybe he'd found someone else to bother. But
I often saw him ride by our house, just to check and see if I
was dead yet, I suppose. I heard that he went to jail just as I
was disappearing, but I'm not for sure. But anyway, since
I'd wanted to be free and enjoy my life and all of the
money that I'd made, the cancer and faking my death plan
was my way out. I'd just needed a way out. Pretending to
die simply solved all of my problems. So, for those few
months I played the part. I offered Mark a good bit of
money, paid everyone in positions to make sure that
everything looked legit, and just like that in the eyes of
everyone…I was dead."

Sonni took a deep breath.

There was so much that had come out of her mouth that it was going to take me a minute to process it all.

I couldn't believe that she'd told such a horrible lie.

And wait a minute…she'd worked at the hotel too? What!

But I'd looked at the women that day or at least I thought that I had.

I guess I hadn't really paid much attention to their actual faces but still I would have noticed my own sister.

I couldn't have seen her.

Maybe she was in one of the rooms that were behind me; the opposite way that we'd gone once we'd gotten off of the elevator that day.

It was just hard to believe.

And Mr. Ben had stalked her too?

Hell, maybe that's why he'd stalked me.

It could have been because I reminded him of her.

My head was starting to hurt and my ears felt as though they were about to bleed.

"Look, maybe it doesn't make sense to you, but this is who I am, what I want and where I want to be. I don't belong there. I don't even want to be there. I just want to be free. And now that I'm supposedly dead…I'm free."

Sonni stood to her feet.

I was trying my best not to cry, but I couldn't help it.

I felt as though she was dying right in front of me.

As though I was watching her being murdered just as I'd watch Tia; but Sonni was doing everything by choice.

This was her choice.

"Do me a favor?" Sonni said grabbing her things.

I simply nodded.

"Don't tell anyone that you saw me. Just let me be," she said.

I nodded again and she smiled.

I felt as though I was going to pass out as she prepared to walk away.

I sat on the bench and she looked back at me.

"Goodbye Envy. Enjoy the rest of your life...*sister*," and with that, she was gone.

There weren't enough hours in the day to explain how I felt at that moment and I wouldn't have dared to even have tried.

I sat there and cried as I watched her until she disappeared.

After a while, finally, I was able to stand and I walked in the other direction.

I glanced by one last time, just to see if maybe she'd turned back around and maybe had second thoughts.

But she was gone.

My mouth started to move but no sound escaped from my lips.

Goodbye Sonni. I love you, sister, I mouthed.

***

As soon as the cab pulled up in front of our house, I noticed the pearl colored Cadillac Escalade, with a big red bow.

I looked over at Silas, who was already looking at me.

"I figured that it was time that you got something new," he said and he helped me with my bags.

I smiled at him and headed towards the car.

I'd never had a brand spanking new car before and as I sat in the driver's seat, I couldn't help but feel as though I'd hit the jackpot with Silas.

Though I had to keep my eye on him, as long as whatever he was into didn't cause me any harm or any issues, I was fine with that.

Maybe he was into drugs or something.

I hope not.

"Do you like it?"

"I love it. And I love you."

Just as we started to kiss, Josephine and her family pulled up to drop off Horizon.

I missed her unexplainably.

She ran to me and I hugged her like never before.

I guess knowing that Sonni never even wanted to see her kids again, made me love and adore Horizon even more.

I hadn't been able to get Sonni off of my mind but I knew that I was going to have to try to forget about her.

She didn't love any of us.

To them she was dead and I secretly had to try to convince myself of the same.

I would never see her again.

I would never hear from her again.

And I just had to get over it and accept it.

Of course I was going to keep my knowledge of her being alive away from Josephine and the others.

There was no point in telling them such horrible news anyway.

So, I was adding another secret to *the list* and hopefully this was going to be the last one.

I just wanted the opposite of what Sonni had wanted.

A normal life.

No secrets.

No lies.

Just love, a husband, kids, family and happiness.

That was all that I needed.

And I was going to have it.

After chatting with my sister and inviting her, Grant and the kids to stay over for take-out, as soon as I could get away, I headed to the bedroom, grabbed the urn and flushed the ashes down the toilet.

Who in the hell ashes were they anyway?

But though I knew that they didn't belong to Sonni, as they disappeared down the toilet, it seemed as though I forced all of the love that I had for her to go down with them.

There was no point in holding on to someone that didn't want to be held on to.

I headed back towards my family, but at the ringing of my cell phone, I stopped in the hallway.

It was Detective Wiley.

"When will you be going back in to the hotel?"

Damn!

No hello.

No how was your trip.

No I'm glad that you didn't drown or die in a plane crash.

Nothing.

Either it was just me or he seemed to want to crack this case as bad as an alcoholic wanted their next drink.

I mean he *really* wanted to take down Carmen, the others and the thirteenth floor.

Maybe it was for recognition or maybe it was for other reasons, but whatever the reasons were, he wanted it so bad that he could taste it.

But still, there was a way of talking to people; especially those that you needed to help you.

Why he gotta' be so rude?

"I'm going in tomorrow. I told her that this was going to be my last week."

"Yeah, well, I'll be the one to make that decision," he said and hung up without bothering to say goodbye.

After it was all said and done, I was going to curse his ass out from here to Mexico.

Detective or not, I was going to let him have it!

Taking a deep breath, I ignored the call from Carmen and headed back to enjoy my family.

Carmen would get plenty of talk time from me tomorrow.

Tonight, I was going to talk to people that I actually wanted to talk to.

"Damn, not one returned call," Carmen said.

I smiled at her but she didn't smile back, so quickly I gave her an excuse.

"I didn't want to be bothered with the phone at all. I just wanted to relax," I said to her, hoping to stay on her good side.

At first she didn't say anything.

She just looked at me.

She looked at me as though she hadn't seen me in years.

After a while, she shrugged and then headed for the inside of the hotel as I followed.

I was so lost in my thoughts that I accidently bumped into one of the maids that were hard at work.

I apologized and she went back to dusting and tending to the plants in the lobby.

I could tell that she hated her job.

I could tell that she was just there to make what little paycheck that she could, just to get by.

I used to be her.

That used to be me.

I'd been in her shoes and I knew exactly how trapped she felt.

Quickly, I glanced at her name tag and continued to follow Carmen to her downstairs office so that we could get on the secret elevator and head up to the 13th floor.

"So, is this still your last week or what? I'll make it where you can only be *reserved* and go ahead and start taking you off the menu," Carmen asked as we got off of the elevator.

I really didn't know how to answer the question.

"I don't know," I answered her.

"Okay, Envy, so why are you still here? We both know that it isn't for the money and I'm sure you are tired of selling your ass to men who don't give a damn about you. So, why are you here?" Carmen asked fiercely.

"I told you. And I guess that I'm just somewhat unsure of what the future really holds. I hate being here, I do. I'm just..." I acted as though I was at a loss for words.

Hell, I knew why I was there but that was my business.

Carmen didn't say anything to my response as we entered her office.

She took a seat and then finally she spoke.

"Okay, well, since you are saying all of that...what about taking over?" Carmen said with no shame at all.

Yeah right!

At least that's what I wanted to say.

Was she stupid?

I definitely didn't want to be in her shoes.

And besides, all of this was about to come to an end.

"Never."

"Why not? You're having a hard time leaving and I have been ready to go for years. It pays more money than you could ever imagine. I'm tired. But it's tricky when it comes to walking away. But if I had a replacement, now that's a different story. And on top of that you know the business and you have been in the game for a while now. *They* would accept you and learn to trust you with no problem. I just need to get away from this place. I just need to live," Carmen said, sounding like a normal person.

But she could sing that tune to someone else, because I already knew what was in store for her and the others, in the near future, so if she wanted to live, she didn't have long to do so.

But then it hit me.

If she thinks that I may consider being her replacement, maybe she would open up a little more.

Maybe she would start saying a few names that could be helpful to the case.

Now, that sounded like a plan.

Just maybe pretending to be onboard with the whole idea just might work.

It just might give me that extra boost to get her to trust me one hundred percent.

Maybe.

I looked at her as she looked at me.

She looked somewhat different for some reason.

For the first time, ever, she looked her age.

Maybe she was serious about being tired, and I'm sure that she was but I wasn't going to be able to help her out on that one.

But for now, I was going to give her just a little hope.

"I don't know Carmen. I mean being in charge…I just don't know. I'll think about it."

The bait was set.

Now, I just had to wait for the fish to bite.

****

Chapter NINE

"Here is your tip *trick*," the man said and left the room.

Maybe it was something in the air, but every new client I'd had lately had been extremely rude and nasty.

If they weren't one of my regulars, they'd been just awful.

I cleaned up the room, but just as I headed out, Carmen burst into the room.

She was crying, and I couldn't believe it.

It was like seeing a hungry lion showing its evening meal sympathy or like a shark deciding to take a day off from biting anything that was close enough to it that he could call lunch.

Basically…it was just very weird for me.

She bum rushed me and forced herself into my chest.

For starters, I was butt ass naked, sweaty, and uncomfortable didn't even begin to describe what I was feeling.

Carmen bawled for all of five minutes and I just stood there.

I didn't pat her back or ask her what was wrong.

I literally just stood there.

After a while she finally pulled herself together and sat on the edge of the bed.

I watched her curiously, waiting for her to say something but instead she started to laugh.

And I mean…laugh.

She was literally laughing.

And it was like a crazy, overly hysterical, creepy kind of laughter.

This bitch is crazy!

Boy I'm telling you, she needed therapy and she needed it right damn now!

"Carmen what's wrong?" I finally asked her in between her laughs.

She continued to laugh and looked in my direction.

"Envy, nothing is wrong."

What?

Oh hell no!

That was my cue to make my exit.

"Come sit and chat with me for a second," Carmen said and patted the bed.

Ugh, but why?

I wanted to go in the opposite direction, out the door that is, but hopeful that she just might say something that I needed to hear, hesitantly I made my way over to her.

I grabbed a dirty towel from the table and attempted to cover up; though my curves and hips had no chance in hell of being hidden.

But at least my breasts and *kitty cat* were concealed.

"Envy, so is tomorrow your last day or should I put you back on the menu?"

I'd had her take me off just in case but I hadn't gotten a thing out of her all week so I knew that I wasn't going to be able to just walk away.

But then again, maybe I could.

The detective didn't have to know that I'd quit.

And the fact that Carmen thought that we were the best of friends, I could still come and visit during the week, just to sit and chat and hopefully find out what he needed to know.

But that was risky.

But…

Hell yeah, that was a chance that I just had to take.

Thinking briefly about my last *lay*, I knew that it was time for me to go.

Mentally, I just couldn't take it anymore.

I just had to go.

And that's exactly what I was going to do.

"Yes. Yes it is. But that won't change our friendship. I'll still come by and see you during the week just to chat. Hell, until all of the plans are up and running for the boutique, I won't have much to do. And since technically you sit around here all day, not doing a thing, I can come bother you, if that's okay," I said, trying to ensure that I would be able to come to the hotel and up to the thirteenth floor, even if I wasn't working, before I made a for sure decision.

Carmen smiled.

"I was worried that you couldn't wait to get away from me," she said.

She was absolutely right but of course I had to keep my thoughts to myself.

"We're friends, now, despite rough beginnings. So hopefully we can stay that way," I said to her and forced a smile.

I was sure that somehow she would find out that it was me that had sold her out but what the hell could she do to me behind bars?

The detective said that they would make the big bust, once everything came together, on a day that I was off from the hotel, so that no one wondered why everyone was going to jail except for me, but since I was really about to call it quits, I guess that wouldn't really matter now.

The only problem with this whole thing was the thought of knowing that no matter how careful we tried to be, I still could be found out.

And especially if I just ended up trying to take what I wanted, then of course Carmen would know that I helped the police get what they needed.

And if there was as much power at the top of the *food chain* as Carmen had mentioned, then there was no telling what kind of connections they had to deal with snitches.

But I couldn't worry about that.

I was promised witness protection if it ever became necessary but if it was done right and I remained discreet, I was hoping that things would be just fine.

I took a deep breath.

I was really going to do this.

I was really going to walk away, finally.

It was time.

Yes, it was time.

"Envy?"

Carmen started to ask but she hurriedly placed her hand over her mouth and headed towards the trash can.

I turned away as she puked.

First she was crying, and then she wasn't, then she was laughing and now she was throwing up.

Hmmm….

"Carmen, are you pregnant?" I asked suspiciously.

She didn't answer me.

She continued to gag for another minute or so and once she stopped, I asked her the same question again.

"Are you pregnant?"

"I don't think so. I'm not sure. I haven't been pregnant in years…"

I could tell that she didn't mean to say the last part of her statement because she stopped abruptly and bit her bottom lip.

She'd been pregnant?

Wow.

She'd never mentioned it before.

"You were pregnant? What happened to the baby?" I asked her.

My gut told me to stop asking questions but my curiosity got the best of me.

"What happened?"

Carmen let out a deep breath and then joined me back on the bed.

"It died."

She didn't have to call it an "it"…but then again she may have not known what the sex of the baby was.

"Oh no, you had a miscarriage?"

"No."

No?

"Well, how did *it* die?"

She looked at me for a while and then she'd had that "oh well, what the hell" moment, and then she opened her mouth.

"*It* died in a car accident."

Wait a minute…what?

What was she trying to say?

"Damn, do I have to spell it out for you Envy? Silas and I had a daughter. And her name was Carmen."

"What? So you mean to tell me that Silas and your sister's daughter, the one that died, and the little girl, Carmen that died, was really your daughter?" I asked her.

She nodded.

What!

What the hell going on around here?

I was so confused.

I was surrounded by liars!

Silas and Carmen had a child?

And then he took her and let her sister raise her as her own?

Huh?

And Carmen allowed it?

Plenty of times she'd referred to the little girl as her niece, so she was going along with the crap and for what?

Why hadn't she ever tried to get her back?

Oh and Silas…he was a dead man!

"I found out that I was pregnant right as we started the divorce proceedings. I was already two months along. I hid it from him until I was too big and started to show. I tried to say that it was someone else's, but he knew that I was lying. So once he found out, he was all over me. He came by my house every single day. I guess he thought that I was going to try to skip town or something. I don't know. He'd said that he was going to be a part of the child's life and that I wasn't going to keep his baby from him. On the day that I had her, I delivered her at the hospital and held her in my arms. That was the only time that I'd ever gotten to I hold her. She was so beautiful. I sent her to the nursery, and when I woke up from a nap, Silas was there. And he was there with court papers. Somehow he and all of his rich buddies had gone back into my past and pulled up a few things that were supposed to be hidden and that he was never supposed to know. They deemed me as mentally incapable of caring for a child. According to them I was unstable and I could potential harm her as well as myself. After I'd killed my father, though my mother took the blame, I'll admit that I wasn't exactly the same or just right after that. I'd spent some time in a couple of hospitals here and there but I was fine. It was nothing a few medications couldn't take care of. I would have been a good mother to my daughter. But Silas had the law and everyone else on his side. He took my daughter from me. He wouldn't even let me say goodbye. Literally two officers basically held me hostage in that hospital room until it was time for me to be released. I should have looked into it. What he'd done and the corners that the people in charge had cut, couldn't have been right, but I didn't even fight. I never saw her again until that day that I spotted her with my sister, the same day of the accident. I'd forced myself to pretend as though she didn't exist the same day I'd walked out of that hospital. It was my way of dealing with it. I didn't try to fight him for her. I never showed up at the court hearings. I just let it be and pretended as though I didn't have a child. I just let them have her. I pretended so much that for years I actually believed the lies that I'd told myself. I didn't even know that he'd named her Carmen like I'd asked him to that day at the hospital until he told me that she was dead. I'd asked him to name her after me. But I thought surely that he wouldn't. But he had. Because deep down, he still had love for me," Carmen said.

I looked at her as she finished her last statement.

Carmen was delusional.

She was just as stupid as she looked.

Silas didn't love her.

Silas had used her to become a citizen.

Plain and simple.

But I wasn't concerned about Silas and everything that she'd just told me.

I was speechless!

No, not my Silas!

He wasn't that type of guy. He just wasn't.

But one thing was for sure and that was that apparently Silas and Carmen had too much history and a ton of secrets that they shared and to be honest, it was too much for me.

Silas was such a good guy around me but obviously Carmen knew the real him and the real him appeared to be ruthless.

How could he take her daughter from her?

Granted, I was right, she was *and* is crazy.

But still, he should have at least attempted to work something out.

You simply don't just take someone's child from them and give them to your new wife---who just so happens to be her damn sister!

I just couldn't believe that he would do something like that.

Maybe Carmen was lying.

She just had to be lying.

Silas was so good with Horizon and he adored the bond that I had with my daughter.

Even when I was tired, he always reminded me to make time for her.

I would never have thought that he would have done something like that to Carmen.

It just didn't make sense.

And Carmen was still secretly obsessed with him after all he'd done to her?

Oh hell yeah, she was just as looney as they came!

With my mind on overload, I didn't say anything to her.

I simply stood up and she stood up behind me.

I headed towards the door in a hurry.

I couldn't wait to get home to confront Silas.

There was no more being quiet.

He had a lot of history and past that was about to mess up his present and his future.

Oh yeah and by the way…the wedding is off!

***

"So, today is your last day at the hotel for sure?" Silas asked.

I hadn't told him what I'd found out at the hotel yesterday only because he seemed to be in a very bad mood when I got home.

He was so angry for some reason or another and he couldn't seem to shake it off the entire evening.

He barely said one word the whole night.

Even when I told him the news about finally leaving the hotel, he'd just nodded his head.

I asked him what was bothering him but of course he wouldn't tell me.

But this morning he seemed to be in a better mood, but I was about to mess it up again.

"Yeah, I am," I answered him nonchalantly.

He walked up behind me and wrapped his arms around my waist.

He inhaled the scent of my skin.

"Why do you always have to smell so damn good just to go clean? And it's your last day, just don't go. Stay here and spend the day with me," Silas said.

I didn't even bother to respond.

Don't worry about what the hell I'm doing...let's talk about you!

"Silas, what do you really do for a living?" I asked.

I figured that I might as well cover all of the basics since I was about to expose yet another one of his secrets.

"I told you. I was smart with my previous riches and I invested wisely. The stock market is where most of my money is tied up in and from dealings with it is where the bulk of my money comes from. Why do you ask Envy?"

"Just to see if I got the same answer," I answered him truthfully.

Silas backed away from me and stood as if he already knew that something else was coming next.

"So, why didn't you tell me that your daughter was actually Carmen's child?"

"She told you that?"

His response wasn't the one I'd thought that it would be.

It kind of caught me of guard a little bit.

"Yes, why?"

Silas didn't respond.

He simply walked away and headed into our walk-in closet.

"Answer me Silas," I said following him, but he was silent.

He looked through his clothes as though he was trying to decide what to wear.

I became so furious at his behavior that I grabbed the closest shoe to me and threw it at the back of his head.

He looked at me with the eyes of an angry tiger, but he still didn't say a word.

"So she was telling the truth Silas?"

I asked him the same question all of ten times but he still refused to give me an answer.

"You know what, either you answer the question or the damn wedding is off!"

With that threat, finally, he looked at me.

Good, that got his attention, but I was serious.

"Yes. Yes she was *our* daughter but Carmen isn't telling you the whole truth. But don't worry about it. I'm going to take care of that," Silas threatened.

Once the words came out of his mouth, it seemed as though I was less mad and more hurt.

I didn't want it to be true.

I really didn't.

I was starting to regret the decisions that I'd made.

Including being with Silas.

And it was the way that he'd said that he was going to take care" of Carmen that told me that he was going to mess Carmen's ass up as soon as he could.

"You say that Carmen didn't tell me the whole story. Well, what's the whole story?"

"Envy, it doesn't really matter. You wanted to know if she was our daughter, yes she was. The rest of the story is irrelevant now."

What right did he have to tell me what was relevant or irrelevant to me?

I wanted answers and I wanted them now!

"Silas you're going to have to say a hell of a lot more than that if you want me to marry you."

Silas gave me another deadly look.

"I can't take anymore secrets. Every time I turn around here comes something else," I said as Silas walked passed me to my side of the closet.

He reached for a duffle bag on the top shelf, unzipped it and threw it at my feet.

"Looks like you have a few secrets of your own," Silas said at the sight of the money spilling out of the bag.

I had two other bags full of money, as well hidden in the house.

Silas was never the messing type so I hadn't overdone it with hiding the money in the house that I'd made from the hotel but I guess I should have.

I'd wanted to put it in a bank account plenty of times, but I feared being questioned as to where it had come from.

"So Envy, you answer some questions. Where is the money from?" Silas asked.

I just looked back and forth between the bag and him.

I didn't know what to say.

"Exactly, so don't come at me about secrets when clearly you have your own. Like I said, I'll take care of it," Silas said exiting the closet and soon exiting the room.

Well, that entire conversation went nowhere, I thought, as I grabbed the small stool and placed the bag of money back on the top shelf of the closet.

I headed to the hotel shortly after, feeling all kinds of confused and frustrated.

I was sick and tired of this *involuntary threesome* of a relationship between Carmen, Silas and myself.

It just always seemed to be something coming up about the two of them or their past.

And I, for one, was over it!

Basically it seemed as though all of Silas's secrets were dealing with, or revolved around Carmen.

I wasn't exactly sure what was going to happen between Silas and I, but I was for sure that I had to get away from the hotel to figure it out.

Carmen greeted me with a smile.

"You've been *reserved* all day," she said.

It was my last day so what the hell.

"By who? Is it a regular?"

Carmen smiled.

"It's by me."

I looked at her.

Now, I wasn't with that funny business.

Carmen was in for a rude awakening if she thought that she was coming anywhere near these curves.

"It's your last day. So, come on," she said, grabbed her purse, and back down the elevator we went.

Oh, I was about to say!

We headed out into the early winter air.

"I'll drive," she said and we headed for her car.

Where in the hell were we going?

To be honest, I still didn't know what was what with what she'd told me the day before and so I felt uncomfortable even being with her.

Maybe she hadn't told the whole story.

Maybe she left something out on purpose.

I didn't know what to believe.

Carmen talked and talked and said that she had to make a quick stop at home before we had a girl's slash supposed to be work, day out.

Once we pulled up at her house, she got out of the car and ran inside.

Her house and the yard even looked adorable in the winter.

It was just so pretty.

I thought about how bad she must feel to have everything but still have nothing.

Then I was reminded that misery loved company.

Maybe she had her own agenda and she wanted to make sure that I ended up just as miserable as she was.

Hey, anything was possible, especially when it came to Carmen.

Maybe she had a few cruel intentions in the works.

I was willing to bet that she did.

I wondered what it was that she was doing and why she was taking so long.

After a few more minutes, I decided to get out of the car.

I decided to walk around her yard.

I wanted to touch everything and just admire it up close.

I felt as though I was in a winter wonderland.

Touching everything in sight, I walked around with a smile on my face.

For some reason the stroll relaxed me.

Before I knew it, I was at the side of the house, checking out a collection of big vases that she had lined up just before you reached one of the side entrances.

Looking at them closely, I could tell that they were very expensive and maybe even hand made.

Carmen definitely had good taste.

Deciding that it was time to head back to the car, I turned around in a hurry and accidently knocked over one of the vases.

Thank goodness that it didn't break.

The dirt, rocks and shells that were in it spilled out but that was about it.

I swatted down to put everything back inside of it, but as I looked closer inside the vase, I saw the corner of what looked to be a stack of papers.

Pulling it out of the dirt, I saw that it was a shit load of papers, held together by a rubber band.

With no hesitation, I grabbed the stack and stuck it up under my arm.

I rushed to fix the vase and then I scurried back to the car.

Once inside, I hurriedly placed the papers in the bottom of my purse.

I didn't know what they were, but they were hidden for a reason.

And I was going to find out why.

Finally, Carmen appeared in the doorway carrying a ton of bags.

I was going to make her carry them all by herself, but I decided to be nice and since I knew that I had the papers in my purse, I was feeling quite jumpy.

I got out and went to help her carry them.

She smiled and handed me a few of them.

I had no idea what she was doing with them.

Maybe they were all returns.

I started towards the car but saw that she still was having trouble so I turned back around to get one more bag from her but…

Bam! Bam! Bam!

And then everything went pitch black.

***

"Hey Mama," I smiled.

Mama smiled at me and soon Tia joined her at her side.

"Hi," they said in unison.

They both looked so beautiful.

I missed them so much that I started to cry.

I tried to walk towards them but they backed away.

I saw my nephew, who was now walking, appear and reach for Tia to pick him up.

She did and I reached for him but he only smiled at me.

I started towards them again, but they backed up again.

They were all smiling but they all started to shake their heads *no*.

I looked at them confused but they only shook their heads no….

I jumped up, gasping for air.

I must have been dreaming.

"Envy calm down. Relax. You're in a hospital," a stranger said.

At the sound of his voice and once I comprehended what he'd said to me, obeyed him and checked out my surroundings.

I was indeed in a hospital.

But why?

Silas appeared seconds later.

He came through the opened door and I could tell that he was more than worried.

"Envy, you were shot in the back, once. Two other bullets grazed you. One grazed your shoulder and one grazed your ear. Can you hear me okay? Tell me if you can feel this."

I could hear him just fine. The doctor touched all over my body and I shook my head yes.

Thank goodness that I could hear and feel.

"Good. We removed the bullet and it looks like you will make a full recovery."

"What happened?"

"We're not exactly sure as of yet, but the police are working on it," he said.

The doctor turned to Silas and smiled before he exited the room.

Silas approached me cautiously.

"Come here," I reached for him.

He looked as though he had been crying but he obeyed me and continued to approach me.

He kissed my forehead and sat beside me.

I smiled at him and held his hand.

What the hell happened to me?

How could I have been shot?

"Silas has anyone said what happened?" I asked him.

He simply shook his head.

The pain seemed to hit me all at once and I whined, causing Silas to look over me as though he was a mama bird hearing the cries of her new baby bird as it cracked open the egg and took its first breath.

Silas tried to make me a little more comfortable, but I had just had a hole in my back, so no matter what he did, nothing worked.

"I'm so sorry this happened to you," Silas said.

And I knew that he meant it.

I could see the love and fright in his eyes.

But I still hadn't forgotten that we weren't on the best of terms.

Just as I opened my mouth to ask a few more questions, there was a knock at the door.

Carmen.

I couldn't quite describe the look on her face.

Maybe she was sad.

Maybe she was worried.

But it also looked as though she was angry.

And I knew why.

It was because Silas was there.

"Just came back to see if you were okay," she said.

"Oh, you were here?"

"Of course. I came in on the ambulance with you. I've been out there waiting for hours,"

I smiled.

Hell, as evil as she was at heart, she could have sat there and watched me die, so I was thankful that she'd actually gotten me help.

Silas didn't speak.

He didn't even look in Carmen's direction.

Instead he told me that he would be right back and exited the room.

"So, it was all a lie? About you and him?" Carmen asked.

This really wasn't the time or the place to talk about the status of my relationship with Silas.

But I knew that Carmen was going to want an answer.

I thought about lying, but I figured that I no longer had to.

I was hoping that whatever it was that I'd found wrapped up in the vase, the papers with the rubber band, was all that I was going to need to get rid of Carmen and my past at the hotel.

"Yes. I knew how you got when we discussed him, so I lied. The truth is we are getting married in April…well, maybe," I said since I wasn't exactly sure what Silas and I were going to do.

Carmen shook her head.

I could see nothing but pure evil on her face.

But with my near death experience, I no longer cared about pleasing anybody else.

"Well, I'm going to go. I'm glad that it was you that got shot. Better you than me. I hate they missed your heart though. Bummer," Carmen said and left without another word.

What?

Who says that to somebody?

Her words were so cruel that they almost made me cry.

Someday, somebody was going to kill that woman.

And then it hit me.

What if Carmen was the one that had me shot in the first place?

It was kind of strange that she'd reserved me for the whole day.

She had taken a mighty long time inside of the house as though she'd known what was going to happen.

Maybe she'd set the whole thing up.

The more I thought about the possibility, the angrier I became.

Sure we had been on pretty good terms since I was pretending to be her friend, but what if she had been pretending the whole time too?

What if?

And if she wasn't behind it all, then who was?

I was so confused and in my feelings that I became emotional.

At the sight of Silas once he reentered the room, I cried even more.

Hell, he was just as hard to figure out as Carmen was.

What if he'd had something to do with it?

We'd just had a big fight.

He'd made a few threats, though they weren't exactly towards me.

How could I be sure that he wasn't behind it all?

Could he really be trusted?

Studying his face, I answered my own question.

Maybe he couldn't be trusted on every single level, but it was clear that he most definitely hadn't shot me or hadn't had someone else to shoot me.

The worry on his face was real.

But someone knew something.

Someone shot me, and someone else knew who it was.

Someone had shot me for a reason.

But why?

****

Chapter TEN

Finally home, I headed to my bedroom to relax.

As soon as I sat on the edge of the bed, my phone started to ring.

"Are you okay?" Detective Wiley asked.

Say it ain't so!

Detective ugly, Mr. Asshole, Rude boy 24/7, was actually asking if I was okay?

I found it funny that he found out that I had been shot but just so happens he hadn't been following me on the day that the incident occurred…right?

Any other day he would have been hot on my trail, especially because I was out with Carmen, but all of a sudden, on that day, he wasn't.

I found that extremely coincidental.

It didn't make sense.

Something just didn't add up.

Something just didn't seem right.

And then again, maybe he was there watching and just didn't do anything.

Maybe he just sat there and watched as I was being shot.

He cared so much about the case against the hotel that I was sure that he would have probably looked on and not have done a damn thing in order to save his case and not blow his cover.

I could definitely see him doing that.

He was so pushy and he wanted to crack this case so bad.

Maybe he wasn't who he said that he was.

I'd never really investigated to see if he was a real detective or not.

I'd just taken his word for it.

What if he wasn't?

After all of this time, just what if he wasn't?

What if he was someone else?

I just didn't know what to think about anyone at this point.

"I'm fine."

"When are you going back to the hotel?"

Of course that's what he wanted to know.

Everyone was all about themselves.

He wasn't concerned that I could have died trying to be friends with someone that I didn't like or want to be friends with in the first place, and it was all for him.

All he cared about was himself.

"What's your badge number?"

"What?"

"You heard me."

After a few more questions, he finally gave it to me and I hung up to call the police station.

Well, the good news was that he was really a detective.

At least he wasn't lying about that, but I still couldn't trust him.

I couldn't trust anyone.

Hell, I could barely trust myself.

I started to call Detective Wiley back to let him know that I had something for him, but I wanted to check it out first.

I found my purse and opened it in a hurry.

I had to see what was on the papers that I'd found in the vase at Carmen's house.

Fumbling around for a while, and after emptying everything out of my huge Prada bag onto the bed, I discovered that the bundle of papers were gone.

What?

I was sure that I had put them there.

So that meant that somebody had to have taken them out.

Who in the hell got them out of my purse?

The only two people that had been around me, that I knew on a personal level, were Carmen and Silas.

Carmen on the way to the hospital, and Silas while I was there.

One of them had to have taken them.

But why?

Obviously those papers would have been my way out but now they were gone.

Things were just getting crazier and crazier, all around me, and I had a bad feeling that something was about to happen.

What in the hell is going on around here?

I was sure that I was about to find out.

***

After two weeks of bed rest and doing nothing, I was feeling a lot better.

 Carmen hadn't called of course, and the detective wouldn't stop calling, so I figured that it was time to make a trip to the hotel.

The detective wasn't exactly happy when I told him about the papers that I'd found, that were now missing.

He agreed that they had gone missing for a reason.

I'd asked Silas if he had gone in my purse at any point in time at the hospital.

I lied and told him that I had some money missing from my wallet and I'd asked him if he had used it maybe at the hospital's cafeteria or something, since he always liked to use cash.

Silas only said no, and that he didn't touch my purse at all.

But someone had.

He promised to call the hospital and make a complaint but I wasn't worried about that.

I was worried about the papers.

But since they were gone, I wasn't going to worry about it.

I was going to the hotel and I was going to *take* the information that the detective needed.

I was done playing around.

I could have died because of it and I was done playing nice.

Silas was all over me but I'd finally convinced him that I was okay enough to go out by myself.

We'd talk over and over again about our relationship and even touched on a few things of the past.

I told him that maybe we should wait on getting married but of course he didn't want to hear that.

He assured me that everything was fine and that he just wanted to forget about his past and not constantly have to relive it.

He told me that Carmen wasn't who I thought she was and that I should stay away from her.

But of course she said the same about him.

Still, I couldn't help but think that with Carmen out of the picture, Silas and I might actually have a chance.

Silas was trying to overdose me with his love and definitely tried to make me see that he was all in.

But I was still confused.

But I was on my way to get some answers.

I pulled up at the hotel.

I was still bandaged but at least everything was working.

The doctors called me lucky, but I saw it as blessed.

Life wasn't through with me yet and I'd be damned if I spent the rest of it behind bars after I'd been spared.

I walked into the hotel and before I headed for Carmen's downstairs office, I looked for the maid named Delilah that I'd bumped into a few weeks ago.

Just so happens, as I stood there looking for her, she came in from behind me and just as she walked in front of me, I called out her name.

She turned to face me.

She looked at me as if she didn't want to be bothered.

I went into my purse and took out an envelope.

I reached it to her.

She took it without hesitating and when she opened it up, she smiled.

"Go home. Follow your dreams." I said to her.

She looked as though she was going to cry but she didn't ask any questions.

"I don't know why, but thank you," she said as she ripped off her name tag, dropped it to the floor and headed back out of the hotel.

The feeling that I felt in the inside was unexplainable.

It felt so good.

I'd given her enough money to last her for a while and hopefully once it ran out, she would be in a better place in life.

It was the least that I could do.

I smiled and headed towards Carmen's office.

My good deed was done, and now it was time to get dirty.

Carmen wasn't in her office and I didn't waste any time getting down to business.

I didn't have any time to look for anything particularly, so I just grabbed papers, a small stack of folders and stuffed them into my purse as quickly as possible.

After snatching everything I could off of her desk, I headed to the drawers below it.

All of the drawers were locked except one of them.

Without bothering to see what was in it, I grabbed what I could, papers, folders, whatever touched my hand, and put it into my purse as well.

Feeling nervous, I was about to turn around and leave but the file cabinet caught my eye.

If she kept sign-on bonus money in there, I was sure that she kept other thirteenth floor related things there.

I opened the top drawer and grabbed everything that I could get my hands on but at the sound of the elevator, I slammed the drawer shut and hurried to the wall in front of the secret elevator and stood directly in front of it.

When the wall pushed open, Carmen looked at me with disgust.

She didn't greet me.

Instead, she walked towards the door.

She looked back to see if I'd followed her and when she saw that I was still standing there, she spoke.

"If you come back on the property, I will have you arrested for trespassing," she said.

I looked at her as though she'd lost her mind but I already knew that she was mad about Silas.

I walked over to her slowly.

"And just so you know, whether you marry him or not, he will always be mine. He still belongs to me. I was the first wife; you'll be his third. But hey if that makes you feel special," she said and literally pushed me the rest of the way out of her office and slammed the door closed behind me.

She locked it as I kicked at it, wishing that I could get to the other side of it and kick her.

All I needed was to smack the crap out of her just one good time.

Just once would give me *life*.

But because I was causing a scene and my body was starting to stiffen up, I headed towards the exit.

Once I was safely in my car, I couldn't wait to see what I'd stolen from Carmen's office.

I was sure that most of the good stuff was in her upstairs office, but it was worth a shot.

I had to have grabbed over a hundred pieces of papers and a few envelopes.

I opened the envelopes and of course they were filled with sign-on bonus money from the file cabinets.

I didn't need the money, so I tossed the envelopes to the side. I focused on the papers.

Looking through the folders and at some of the papers, I saw that I'd managed to grab some stuff that definitely might be helpful.

There were papers with years of personal information and identification of women that had come through the thirteenth floor.

My name was on a page or two as well as some of the other girls that only worked the thirteenth floor; which confirmed that the information that I was looking at was in regards to the *executive maids* and not the regular ones.

I scanned the pages as fast as I could, looking for something---something big.

There was nothing extremely useful in that set of papers, so I dug out more crumbled pages from my purse and started to go through them.

Just as I seemed to be headed toward something good, the knock on my car window almost made me piss on myself.

"Open the door Envy."

It was Carmen.

Oh, so she wanted to be bad huh?

Just as my hand touch the door handle, so that I could get out and give her a run for her money, messed up back and all, Carmen spoke.

"So, you want to come in my office and steal money from me? Open the door bitch," Carmen said.

I paused and looked at her.

Damn it.

Why hadn't I pulled off?

Instead of opening the door, I started my car instead.

At the sound of the engine, out of nowhere Carmen swung a fairly large piece of wood at my driver's side window, shattering it instantly.

This crazy ass bitch!

I hadn't even seen the wood in her hand.

Still talking, she smashed the backseat window out next.

Barely able to focus, I put the gear in drive and sped off.

I drove and I didn't stop driving until I was in the parking lot of the police department.

At that point, I attempted to remove the glass from my hair and various places on my body.

Oh, she was going to pay for this.

Whether with her *beat ass* or with her life, she was going to pay.

I was so mad that all I could see was red, but I had to focus.

I had to keep it together.

Carmen was going to get hers, one way or another.

My phone started to vibrate, back to back, from calls from Carmen.

I didn't bother to answer it.

I grabbed the papers instead.

Still in frenzy, I started to look at the papers again.

Loads of information about the maids, clients, and payments, but I was looking for more.

It wasn't until I was down to my last twenty or so pieces of paper, that I finally I saw something.

I saw a whole lot of something.

And then…

I saw something else.

My mouth opened wide and I couldn't believe my eyes.

Oh my Goodness!

That bitch!

***

Though I was supposed to stay at home, I sat across from the hotel.

I wanted to see the big bust go down.

I'd handed over the necessary papers to the detective and with all of the information that was on them, he was finally able to make his move.

I had been granted freedom as promised and I was in the clear.

I thought that when this day came, if it ever came, I would feel nervous and maybe even a little bad for playing the part of sending so many folks to jail and even prison, but somehow, I didn't feel bad at all.

I was angry.

That's the only emotion that I felt.

I was angry enough to get crazy.

Not Carmen's kind of crazy…but ghetto, ratchet kind of crazy.

And I had my reasons.

I watched the detective and his men head into the hotel.

People, regular maids and employees scurried out of the hotel and flooded the sidewalk, unsure of what was going to happen next.

I decided to get out of the car and join the crowd.

To be honest, I just wanted to see the look on Carmen's face.

I wouldn't have to testify or anything.

The documentation had everything that they you could think of on it from names, payouts, sponsors and so much more.

They had all the proof that they needed and they were sure that when plea bargains started to float around that they would get even more information.

They offered to place me and my family in witness protection once again.

But I didn't think that we would need it.

I was sure that Carmen noticed the missing paperwork, but then again, maybe she only noticed the opened file cabinet and thought that I was simply trying to steal.

Who knows and who cares!

Of course I hadn't spoken to her, so I had no idea what she was thinking.

After she'd busted my windows with the wooden plank, she called over a hundred times.

I never answered so I was sure that I was going to see her later on that day.

Carmen knew where I lived, and I just knew that she was going to bring the drama to my home.

And I waited on her all night too.

I just knew that she was going to pop up and run right into an ass whooping, but she didn't come.

She finally stopped calling, and she never came.

That definitely made me curious.

Why wouldn't she have come?

And the more I thought about it, and because Carmen was part stalker, I wondered if she'd ever saw the detective and I meet up on the few occasions that we'd met in person to exchange information.

Thinking about it, I was almost sure that she had.

And I was willing to bet that she'd pulled whatever strings that she had to in order to find out who he was, so now I was really wondering as to whether or not Carmen had something in the works or not.

Did she know about the detective?

Did she know what I was up to all along?

Did she have a plan?

But whether she did or not, today, her ass was going to jail.

Seconds later, there they were.

The maids on duty, on the thirteenth floor, came out in handcuffs.

Most of them were wearing bed sheets.

They could have at least allowed them to put on some clothes.

After a few more minutes, Detective Wiley finally made his exit and it was as if he'd spotted me immediately.

The look on his face said that he was upset that I disobeyed his orders, but he turned his back to me and stood directly in front of me as though he was trying to ensure that Carmen or any of the others didn't get a view of me.

Soon after, and though I had to move around and hide behind a few people, Carmen came out.

Strangely she was smiling as the crowd grew louder and everyone started to ask questions.

She was smiling as though she'd won some type of award or something.

They led her to a patrol car and put her inside.

I watched the officers as they spoke briefly to Detective Wiley and then they finally headed back to their cars and at the same time, all of the police cars with the maids and Carmen inside of them, pulled off and started down the road.

I watched the car that Carmen was in and just as it was passing by, Carmen turned, looked directly at me and winked.

What the hell!

She knew!

As soon as they were out of sight, Detective Wiley turned around and spotted me.

He walked over to me as though he was a parent about to discipline their child.

"I told you to stay at home."

"I know, I just wanted to see the look on her face. She was smiling, did you see that?"

He nodded.

The smiling made me wonder but the wink had me freaked out.

But for some reason, I didn't mention it to the detective.

"We have officers heading to pick up all of the folks that we could locate from the paperwork. We will be making a lot of arrests," Detective Wiley said.

I was still stuck on Carmen and her actions.

Something just didn't sit right with me.

"Why was she smiling?" I asked aloud again, although I meant to ask myself the question internally.

Something told me that she was up to something.

I just knew that she was up to something.

"She won't be smiling for long. I finally got her. I told her that I was going to get her and I finally got her," he said.

What?

What the hell was he talking about?

So he knew Carmen?

And he told her that he was going to catch her?

Huh?

I knew that something wasn't right about him and this case!

I knew it!

"What are you talking about? I knew that you were too attached to this case. I knew that there was a reason that you wanted to bring down the operation so badly. Why?"

He looked at me.

He was hesitant at first, but then he spoke.

"My best friend, and partner when I was just a cop, had an affair on his wife with Carmen. It was a while ago. Their relationship wasn't hotel related but he'd snooped through her phone a time or two while she was sleeping and found out that the hotel had other business that she was a part of. Anyway, whatever they had was just sex. I didn't judge because it wasn't my business. His personal life wasn't my business. The fact that he was cheating on his pregnant

248

wife, wasn't my business. He complained that his wife was fat and pregnant and she didn't want to have sex as often as he did, so he had Carmen to take care of those needs. He promised that once the baby was born, that things between them would be over."

He paused for a second to answer the phone.

As soon as he hung up, he continued.

"But as the story goes, he and his wife had been intimate just a few times during her pregnancy. I guess whenever Carmen was unavailable. But it wasn't until the baby was born that she found out that both of them were HIV positive. Carmen had given him HIV and he'd taken it home to his wife and son. Though his wife had been tested a few times during pregnancy, it hadn't shown up until after delivery. My best friend, Jay, tested positive too. He knew that he had only been with one other woman and that was Carmen. He went to her and told her the news and when he told her, he said…she laughed. He said she laughed in his face. He'd said that she laughed so hard that tears came out of her eyes and then she'd said…that she already knew. Can you believe that? She knew she'd ruined his life and she even knew that he had a pregnant wife at home but she hadn't cared. She hadn't cared. She'd given him the disease and blamed him for being a cheating husband. So, Jay had to tell his wife about his transgressions and being that she said she was leaving him and that she would never forgive him and because he couldn't forgive himself, he committed suicide. Just like that he was gone. But on the day of his funeral, I told her, Jay's wife, my godson's mother, that if it was the last thing I do, I was going to get her. I told her that I was going to get Carmen in any way that I could and that she was going to pay for what she had done. You don't just ruin people life because you feel like it. Jay wasn't exactly in the right either but what Carmen had done was just unspeakable and I dedicated myself to putting her behind bars. So, I'd tried to hit her with an attempted murder charge since she'd known that she was sick and passed it on, but no one would file the charges. It seemed as if the entire police department was afraid to make a move on her. I mean it was as though they were terrified or all being paid to let her do as she pleased. I was just a cop back then but I vowed that I was going to get her. And I knew that I was going to have to go after the hotel to do it. So, once I was promoted to detective and after finally getting some people to have my back on this, I got to work. And I did it," he said.

No, *I* did it.

He didn't do a darn thing.

But I couldn't believe all of the things that he'd just said.

A lot of it left me speechless, but for the most part, I just hoped that Carmen got what she deserved.

Carmen was low down and dirty and she deserved to pay.

And she was HIV positive?

Never!

Ninety-five percent of the time she looked amazing, stunning, and far from dealing with something of that nature.

But looks could be deceiving.

Of course she had the money and the means to get nothing but the best treatment so I was sure that she kept up with her medication I suppose.

I mean seriously, that was just something that you would have never been able to tell unless she told you.

And that was something that she'd definitely kept to herself.

Now the question was, where had she gotten it from and how long had she had it?

Immediately I thought about Silas but I'd been tested plenty of times since I'd been at the hotel, since it was a requirement, so I knew that my health was intact; which in turn meant that Silas was fine too.

And then again, HIV was known to lay dormant in some cases…

No, I wasn't even going to allow myself to think about anything like that.

I was fine and so was my health.

I hated that the wife and the child had to suffer because of the actions of Carmen and her husband, but I was learning daily that every action came with a consequence…even when it came to a few actions of my own.

"So, you used me?"

"I helped you. Whether it was you or another one of the maids, either way, I wouldn't have stopped until Carmen was in my custody. Are you sure you don't want witness protection?" Wiley asked.

I shook my head no.

Hopefully I was making the right decision.

"Envy?"

I looked at him as to ask *what*.

But he shook his head.

"Never mind. Thank you," he said.

"And thank you. I'm free," I said and turned away from him, making my way to the car.

I didn't pull off right away.

I was so emotional.

That could have been me coming out of there in handcuffs.

That could have been me going to jail along with the rest of them.

I was so grateful that I couldn't even express my gratitude if I tried.

I hadn't gone down with the *Hush Hotel* and even though I should have, it was in the divine plan that I didn't.

So though I'd made an awful choice, I was now able to start fresh.

And that Carmen, well, she was even crazier than I'd thought that she was, but she would have years to think about the decisions that she'd made and hopefully she would release whatever it was that made her so damn evil.

She was just pure damn evil.

I wondered how many other men she'd done something like that to and how many other families she'd destroyed.

But who was I to even go there.

Hell, I'd ruined families and marriages too.

I sat there for a while longer and watched the crowd as they either walked away or made their way back inside the hotel.

I was surprised that they hadn't shut the entire thing down, but I was sure that it was coming soon.

The streets were clear, so finally I decided to head home.

I had a long drive so I planned to use it to really get my thoughts together.

My mind was racing and my heart was pounding so fast that I thought that it was literally going to *beat* me to death.

It was so much to take in and what happened at the hotel wasn't even the half of it.

Thoughts filled every empty space of my head and I tried to get my mind together.

I couldn't wait to get home to Silas.

I pulled up to my house and before the car was even fully in park, I was out of the car heading for the front door.

Silas was sitting on the couch and immediately stood as he read my body language.

I walked over to him and hugged him.

"What's wrong?"

What isn't was the question.

"Is everything okay?"

I shook my head.

I reached into my purse and handed him a few papers that I *hadn't* turned in to the detective.

Silas looked at me.

And I looked at him.

"So should I call you Silas, baby…or *Boss*?" I asked him.

Yep that's right.

Silas was one of the *top dogs* of the thirteenth floor and had been the whole time.

Ain't that a bitch!

Oh, but it gets worse.

Silas was at the top, but there was someone bigger.

And it wasn't Carmen.

The big *Boss* of the whole operation was…

To be continued…

Text TBRS to 95577 to be notified when book three, the finale, is being released!

CPSIA information can be obtained at www.ICGtesting.com
Printed in the USA
LVOW08s2136300715

448258LV00001B/256/P